BETWEEN WORLDS 7

WHAT WILL COME

LORI WOLF-HEFFNER

HEAD IN THE GROUND PUBLISHING

ISBN (Paperback Edition) 978-1-989465-15-8

ISBN (Ebook Edition) 978-1-989465-16-5

ISBN (Large Print Edition) 978-1-989465-17-2

Some characters and events in this book are fictitious. Any similarity to real persons, living or dead, is coincidental and not intended by the author.

Editing by Susan Fish

Cover design by Fresh Design

All photographs from Shutterstock

Head in the Ground Publishing

Waterloo, Ontario, Canada

headintheground.com

❀ Created with Vellum

To Jean Little (January 2, 1932 – April 6, 2020), whose writing has influenced my own in more ways than I'm sure I know.

CHAPTER ONE

"*J*uliana!" Mom called.

Juliana closed the book she was reading for English and sighed. "I'm coming!" she replied from her bedroom. She had a pretty good idea of what Mom wanted. But with the semester already half over, fixing things was out of the question.

The floor creaked with each step Juliana took toward the house's small kitchen. To her surprise, though, she was greeted by an outburst of laughter from her mother and grandfather.

Opa wore black pants, a white shirt, and a black, button-down vest. Juliana hadn't seen this outfit before; her grandfather preferred browns and beiges, not crisp blacks and whites. A rose corsage was pinned on one side of his vest. A green crest of some kind was sewn on the other side, with kitschy souvenir pins filling the area around it.

Opa slapped his hand on the table. "Karl told such a funny joke," he said to Mom, who was laughing with him. "It was only something you understood if you worked in the rubber factory. It was so funny!"

Mom leaned back in her chair at the kitchen table, her face relaxing into a smile. Her posture didn't at all match the voice that had called Juliana only moments ago. Had Juliana heard right?

"So your seventy-first birthday party at the club was fun, then?" Mom asked.

Opa threw his hands in the air. "Katy, it was so much fun! We laughed, sang the old songs..."

"And drank some beer?" There was a twinkle in Mom's eye.

Opa's face turned serious. "But not too much, Katy. I remember what the doctor said about my medicine."

Mom nodded and seemed satisfied with Opa's response. Juliana smiled. She loved seeing her grandfather happy like this. They had served a birthday breakfast for him as a family this morning, and Mom, Dad, and Juliana gave Opa a flat-screen television and something unique: Mom called it a tab. Anytime Opa wanted to eat with his friends at the café in Belmont Village, a small shopping strip across the street, Mom and Dad would pay. Opa had at first refused what he thought was such an expensive gift, but Mom and Dad had insisted.

"Every generation of Schuhmachers goes there," Mom had explained. "Casimiro and his wife are such good people, and I know you like the German club, but this way, you can call a friend or two, and they can meet you there, and you don't have to wait for me or Annie to drive you."

Opa had squeezed each one of them tight in his arms.

Now, after Opa's fun afternoon at the German club, both Mom and Opa were laughing. Their unexpected happiness eased Juliana's apprehension about why Mom had called her.

"Oh, there you are," Mom said, spotting Juliana. Her smile disappeared.

Juliana's hopes vanished.

"Tata, do you mind if we talk about this some more later? Right now, I have to talk with my daughter. Besides, you should get out of your *tracht* so it doesn't get dirty."

Juliana didn't recognize the German word Mom said to Opa, but she certainly recognized the tone Mom used with her. It was the one Juliana had been expecting.

Opa stood up. "Yulika, you should have seen the women—some wore their dirndls to my party." Opa always called her Yulika, and although the nickname had bothered Juliana when she first moved in, she'd come to cherish it now. No one else called her that except him.

"But Barbara wore her *tracht,*" he said, pausing at the

doorway to the basement. He smiled mischievously at Mom. "I still think she likes me. She even gave me this flower." He pointed to the corsage.

Mom broke out into laughter again, and Juliana hoped she'd forget why she'd called Juliana in the first place.

"Is Yulika in trouble?" Opa asked.

Juliana lost any chance of getting out of the impending talk.

"It's between me and Juliana, Tata."

Opa walked down the two steps to the landing and turned back. "She's still young, Katy. Be nice. You were a girl once, too."

Mom's shoulders stiffened. "And you got angry at me when I didn't do well."

"I'm sure you would still have become a good person if your *modr* and I had been nicer to the three of you." Opa disappeared around the corner as he headed to his bedroom in the basement, leaving Juliana alone with Mom.

Mom lost no time. She crossed her arms and the expression on her face showed she meant business. "Belinda at work today said that her son got his report card over a week ago. Your father and I haven't seen yours. Where is it?"

Juliana stared at the carpeted kitchen floor. "We don't have to get our parents to sign report cards," she said, knowing full well that Mom wouldn't buy her excuse.

"That's not what I asked, Juliana Elizabeth Roth. Where is your report card?"

Juliana dragged her feet back to her bedroom, reached to the bottom of her backpack, and pulled out a ball of paper. She returned to the kitchen and handed it to Mom.

Anger clouded Mom's face. "We've been through this before. Your father and I know you've been going through a lot since we moved here, but we still expect you to be honest with us." While Mom unfurled the crumpled report card carefully to avoid ripping it, Juliana kept her eyes focused on the floor, the dark brown and black threads turning into abstract patterns. As she shifted her weight from one side to the other, the floor squeaked, tempting her to create a rhythm with the sound. But that would anger Mom even more right now.

"If you would tell me and your father more often when things are too hard for you, we could try and help you." Mom scanned the report card. "You're close to failing science!" Mom looked up, though there was no anger in her face. It was worse than that. Juliana saw disappointment. She felt the same way about herself.

Mom returned her eyes to the report card. "'Often looking at her phone...she's a bright girl but is encouraged to study more...'" She shook her head. "Sweetie, you can do better than this. Much better. On top of it, you probably already learned some of this material in Calgary. Your father and I obviously understand what happened last semester. But now? How can your marks not have returned?"

Mom and Dad never expected top marks from their daughter: Juliana had always been motivated to keep her marks high. Back in Calgary, she had been in junior high, which meant she took most subjects all year long, not four in one semester and four in the next one, like they did in high school here in Ontario. Because they had moved to Kitchener over Christmas, Juliana had had to cram hard to write three exams in January. She had passed, but with lower marks than she was used to. Much lower marks. But even when the new semester began, she couldn't bring herself to study. With the semester now almost halfway over, she wondered why bother starting? Besides, more important things demanded her attention.

They had moved to Kitchener because Opa had Alzheimer's. Juliana had barely known him when they arrived, but now she really wanted to. Jasmine, her new best friend at dance, had encouraged Juliana to talk more often to Opa before it was too late. At school, another new friend, Meghan, had suggested Juliana focus on dance because you can't be a dancer when you're older but you can go to university at almost any age. This made sense to Juliana, who loved talking with Opa and practising dance, especially tap.

"As I said," Mom continued, "I know things have been really hard. It's exactly why we only wanted you doing four dances this year at your new studio instead of your usual eight or ten. Judging by these marks, it was the right decision. I almost wish your dad hadn't allowed you to join the dance club at school. Is there anything you're having an especially hard time with? Do you need a tutor? Have you talked to your guidance counselor?"

Juliana shook her head. She understood everything fine and always turned her homework in. But come study time, her mind would wander and she would find herself wondering about Elisabeth—Opa's mother—and Opa's disease. Although the move had given Juliana the family she never had in Calgary, she still felt alone in dealing with many of the challenges she faced. She appreciated Mom's offer of help right now, but it seemed like an empty offer.

Mom had once taken Juliana to see an Alzheimer's counselor along with her cousin Sophie and Aunt Anne. The session had really helped Juliana and her twelve-year-old cousin understand how Opa's brain was changing. But later, when Juliana wanted to talk to the counselor alone about Opa *and* Mom, she couldn't get there or pay for the appointment without her parents knowing.

Things at home had begun to improve recently, with moments like Mom and Opa laughing together. But it had been very recent. Certainly not long enough to help Juliana focus on her marks again.

Mom looked at her watch. "I promised my manager I'd give him a quick call in five minutes."

Mom's work again. *Things haven't changed, I guess,* Juliana thought.

"Are you sure there's no way I can help?" Mom asked. "You've told me and your dad a few times that you've felt alone, and we're both really sorry. But until we can get things at work better under control, we're more than happy to find other people to help you."

"Mom, I'm fine. I don't need the help." Juliana actually meant she didn't *want* the help. Was that a lie? She added, "The problem in science is that our homework counts less than our tests. I just have to study more, that's all."

Mom studied Juliana up and down and sighed. "All right, then. But your father and I are going to keep an eye on you. I want you to promise me that you will do better. I know you can, and I know you'll feel better if those marks get up. It's tempting to want to keep practising, especially after what I saw at competition this weekend: you have improved so much in these last few months that I hardly recognize you on stage anymore. I'm sure you're dying to keep it up. But school is what's going to get you through life, not dance, okay? You know I'm speaking from experience here."

Juliana sighed and nodded. "I promise."

Mom seemed to accept Juliana's promise. Mom took her purse from the kitchen table and headed to her bedroom, the only place where she could have a semi-private conversation in Opa's small bungalow. But before she closed the door, she said, "Don't forget next Sunday. We're celebrating Easter and Tata's birthday. Uncle Peter will be back from France, so it works for everyone." Mom closed the door.

Julianna returned to her room and pulled out her great-grandmother's old, leather-bound sketchbook. Juliana privately called her great-grandmother by her first name—Elisabeth—because her great-grandmother had begun to feel more like a friend to her. Juliana had only learned last month that her middle name was her great-grandmother's name, with a slight variation in spelling. But Mom and Dad had never told her *why* they'd chosen Elizabeth for a middle name. *Why the secret?* she thought. *From what Opa's told me, Elisabeth was an amazing person.*

Juliana returned her attention to the sketchbook. Elisabeth had drawn these pictures when she was Juliana's age, almost a hundred years ago. The stories Opa remembered about some of the drawings intrigued Juliana, and she loved asking him about them. Other drawings didn't seem to have a story—for example, Opa didn't know why Elisabeth had drawn a lantern—but even those pictures somehow spoke to her. To Juliana, that lantern helped her understand how her own anger flowed through her body when she danced.

"I wonder what today's drawing is?" she said aloud. She tried to look at only one new drawing each time she opened the sketchbook. "I could really use a friend right now."

Juliana paged past drawings of an old kitchen without a phone, hands trying to pull off mittens from another pair of hands, and members of a family sitting at a table. She stopped at the first unfamiliar drawing she came across. Juliana tried not to page ahead because she assumed that Elisabeth would have drawn these in chronological order, as they happened. Juliana and Dad had once found a drawing of a burial deeper in the book, and thankfully Opa didn't know the name of the man in the open coffin. She wanted to wait until she got to that drawing to find out.

She stopped at a drawing of a cracked egg sketched in pencil. Because it was sketched in gray pencil, Juliana couldn't tell if it was a coloured egg. Based on her last conversations with Opa, this sketch had probably been drawn around Easter. The previous two drawings depicted memories from Elisabeth's confirmation, the ceremony when she became an adult in her church. According to Opa, that always happened one week before Easter, on Palm Sunday. Whatever the story behind this egg drawing, it expressed how Juliana felt: like she was cracking.

CHAPTER TWO

*E*lisabeth lifted the lid off the pot of boiling water.

"They look done," she mumbled to herself and removed the pot from the brick-and-lime wood stove and placed it on a hot plate on the wooden kitchen table. She lifted each hard-boiled egg out with a spoon and set it on a tea towel, leaving the onion skins in the water. She marvelled at the lovely reddish-brown colour the skins had dyed the eggs and was happy to have prepared at least this much for Easter.

A few groans signaled to Elisabeth that one sibling was stirring. *Sounds like Rosina*, she thought. Rosina was six, the youngest of the four Schuhmacher children. Elisabeth, at fourteen, was the eldest.

While the eggs cooled, Elisabeth sliced cheese. Rosina stumbled out of the front room, where the entire family slept, and Elisabeth wished her a cheerful happy Easter. However, Rosina seemed too tired to get excited about the day.

Or maybe she's still sad about yesterday, Elisabeth thought. Mammi had become so ill that the midwife and Margarethe-Néni, Elisabeth's aunt, had come to care for her while the Schuhmacher children spent the rest of the day at their aunt and uncle's house. Elisabeth had lied to Rosina, Anna, and Luki, saying that Mammi was very sick. They were too young for the truth.

Boiling and colouring the eggs this morning, and a little cleaning yesterday, were the only signs that Easter celebrations were underway in the Schuhmacher household. She hadn't even killed and prepared a goose for Easter dinner after church.

"Is Mammi going to feel better today?" Rosina asked, rubbing her eyes.

Elisabeth shrugged and asked Rosina to pull down plates from the shelf to set the kitchen table. She didn't know what the day would bring, so she wanted to keep the dining table in the back room clean. Just in case. Most years, the Schuhmachers enjoyed Easter lunch as a family —sometimes with extended family and sometimes alone— and then visited relatives all afternoon. Other times, family would visit them for a light supper, having been filled during the day by delicious Easter meals with other family members. Eating in the dining room only happened if they had guests.

Plates clanged together as Rosina lifted them down from the shelf one by one. Elisabeth admonished her to be quiet lest she wake up Mammi. Rosina's lip quivered and Elisabeth feared she had overreacted.

"I'm sorry," Elisabeth said, rushing over to help her sister with the plates. "I guess I feel sad because we won't have much of an Easter today. Why don't you go wash up? I'll finish setting the table."

Rosina nodded and dragged her feet over to the washing bowl, which sat on a table in a corner of the kitchen. Elisabeth had filled it with fresh water from the well first thing that morning, hoping it would come to room temperature before anyone needed it. Rosina washed her face and neck with a cloth and no complaint. Elisabeth then directed her to sit at the table, where Elisabeth had also set a cup of peppermint tea and a cup of water.

"But be careful, it's hot," Elisabeth said. "Drink some water for now if you're thirsty."

"Are we going to hunt for eggs?" Rosina asked.

Elisabeth shook her head, wishing now she had awoken early enough to cook the eggs and hide them outside. But the day before had exhausted her so much that waking up to make breakfast was the best she could do.

"Is it because Mammi was sick?"

Elisabeth nodded. "But I'm sure she'll be better soon."

It's all right to lie to make someone feel better, isn't it, Jesus? she asked the figure on the crucifix on the wall.

"But the Easter rabbit would make Mammi happy," Rosina offered. "I think he should still come."

Elisabeth needed to change the subject. What none of her siblings knew was that Mammi had lost a baby. The Easter rabbit could not make Mammi happy. "But the Easter rabbit also knows that Mammi needs her rest," Elisabeth said.

Rosina stared at her cup of water, her drooped shoulders tugging at Elisabeth's heart.

"What about *titschen*?" Elisabeth asked and Rosina's eyes brightened. "If we have eggs left over from breakfast, we'll keep them in the cellar, and we can do *titschen* this afternoon or evening. Does that sound all right?"

Smiling, Rosina nodded. Elisabeth breathed a sigh of relief. She had succeeded at her first challenge: distracting Rosina from the Easter rabbit's absence by reminding her about their traditional egg-tapping competition. But a much larger challenge loomed ahead: how would Mammi be today?

Mammi had lost two babies before this one: Anna's twin had been stillborn, and a baby had been born before Elisabeth. Georg, a cousin from Margarethe-Néni's family who was only five years younger than Mammi, had told Elisabeth the day before that Mammi had become easier to anger after losing each one. He didn't say any more than that, but Elisabeth could guess what he meant. The same had happened after Tata's departure in November for America, and Mammi became angrier still as the baby grew inside her. Although Mammi never hesitated to punish her children for bad behaviour, she seemed to do it more often now, even more than she had during the war.

Tata had been home during those sad times. He must have helped Mammi. Was that not Elisabeth's duty now? Georg had also told Elisabeth she needed to push past Mammi's anger and keep the family together. But how would she do that?

"Elisabeth!" Mammi called from the front room.

"Are you feeling better?" Rosina said, running in ahead of Elisabeth.

"Out!" Mammi commanded. "And the two of you, too!"

Elisabeth's two other siblings, Luki and Anna, rubbed their eyes as they crawled out of bed.

"Now!" Mammi said.

Luki scrambled out the door while Anna fumbled for her crutches—she had sprained her ankle the week before when some boys had pushed her after teasing her about Tata working in America. Tata had moved away four months ago, but it felt like four years to Elisabeth.

"Wash up," Elisabeth gently called out after them. "We'll have breakfast shortly."

"Close the door," Mammi said. Elisabeth did as she was told. Mammi's face was pale and her lips were pulled into their usual tight line. "Reach me those." Mammi pointed to a stack of old sheets, and Elisabeth followed Mammi's instructions. "Now turn around."

Elisabeth turned her back to Mammi. Mammi grunted and groaned, and sheets rustled.

"Can I help—?"

"I said turn around, or didn't you hear me?"

Her voice almost too weak to pass her lips, she replied, "I heard you, Mammi." This was what Georg meant.

Elisabeth waited until Mammi asked her to face her again.

Mammi kept her voice low. "The children do not know what happened yesterday, do they?"

Elisabeth shook her head.

"Good. See to it that it stays that way. They're too young to understand."

Elisabeth nodded.

Mammi handed her a large bundle of sheets.

"Take these out to the summer kitchen and soak them in cold water. Later today, they will need to be washed."

Elisabeth stared at the bundle, worried about what made them so dirty. But she pushed her worries down. "Is there anything else I can help with?"

"Get me a glass of water, then get the children ready and take them to church."

"But—"

"Elisabeth Schuhmacher, do not—" Mammi dropped

forward as she wrapped an arm around her middle and tried to repress a cry.

Elisabeth touched Mammi's shoulder but Mammi jerked it off. A moment later, Mammi's body relaxed. She took several deep breaths before speaking. Her voice was firm but she didn't make eye contact with Elisabeth. "Make sure the children are spotless. I do not want to give Meier Josef something more to gossip about. Frau Molnár has probably already told him about the baby."

In their Lutheran congregation, everyone from the church gossip—Meier Josef—to the midwife—Frau Molnár—shared stories about everyone else. Everyone's business became everyone's business. When Tata was home and was making or repairing shoes in the workshop out back, Mammi would be ready at the door with a spoon or belt to spank Luki if he had caused trouble along the way home from school. Word would already have reached Mammi.

Someone knocked on the house door in the kitchen and a moment later Margarethe-Néni entered the front room. Although it was Sunday, Margarethe-Néni wore a regular skirt, apron, leather slippers, and tucked-in blouse, and not her black Sunday clothes, suggesting she planned to stay here instead of attend the Easter service at church.

"Lissa, Lissika," she said to Mammi and Elisabeth. "Happy Easter."

Mammi and Elisabeth responded in kind. Elisabeth

appreciated the kind—though expected—words rather than her aunt's customary way of finding an opportunity to insult her family.

"Margarethe, I told you not to come," Mammi said as she pulled her sheets over her body and lay back down. Mammi did not say those words out of politeness. She was being honest: she didn't like anyone in Tata's family.

Margarethe-Néni took the sheets out of Elisabeth's hands. "This is why I've come. Your daughter should not be washing these. Your mother is on her way. She can help with the cooking. Frau Molnár is coming, too, so she can see how you're feeling. I'll get you a cup of water." She promptly carried the sheets outside.

"Join your siblings," Mammi said to Elisabeth, her lips barely moving out of their straight line. "Their Sunday clothes are in the back room, as always. Take washcloths and stockings out of here and leave me alone."

Elisabeth nodded. As she collected the items she needed, she realized that doing what Mammi told her to do would help Elisabeth look past Mammi's anger and keep the family together.

Her aunt returned, cup of water in hand, and the midwife behind her. "Leave us," Margarethe-Néni told Elisabeth as though Elisabeth needed Mammi's command repeated. Washcloths and stockings collected in her apron, Elisabeth hurried out of the front room and closed the door behind her.

"Why are they here?" Anna asked.

"To help Mammi get better," Elisabeth answered.

"But Mammi doesn't like Margarethe-Néni. None of us do. How can she help Mammi get better?"

Elisabeth shushed Anna. "You don't talk like that about someone! Especially when they're here!" At the same time, Anna often saw things logically and Elisabeth did agree with her. *Mammi must be all right with her here, because otherwise she would make sure Margarethe-Néni left.* What Elisabeth didn't understand, though, was why Mammi's two sisters weren't coming to help. *Maybe they'll be coming with Omama a little later?* Omama must have told them.

Only now did Elisabeth notice that her sisters and brother had begun eating.

"You didn't wait for me?"

"We were hungry," Luki said.

Elisabeth threw her hands up in exasperation and sat down. She had placed a slice of buttered bread on her plate when there was another knock at the door. Elisabeth let Omama in.

As usual, Omama didn't have a smile on her face either. "You're to get your sisters and brother ready for church," she instructed Elisabeth.

If anyone else told Elisabeth about her duties toward her family, she was going to crack. *That was the third time,* she thought. *I've been in charge of my family since the new year. I know my duty.*

Omama shuffled in, followed by Peter-Bátschi, her son and Mammi's only brother to survive the war, carrying a suitcase. Omama directed him to set it in the back room, on the other side of the kitchen. Elisabeth's jaw dropped in horror. Was Omama staying? Even the looks on her siblings' faces told Elisabeth that they worried about that, too.

The last time Omama Braun had stayed, she had spanked Luki and almost forced Elisabeth to hit her brother so he would obey. The memory reminded Elisabeth of yesterday, when she had lost her patience with Luki under the strain of Mammi's miscarriage and had actually struck him. Her heart still ached. Elisabeth didn't understand how parents and grandparents hit their children so often without regret. Besides, Jesus didn't hit children, so why did adults?

"Now go back to your family," Omama instructed her son.

Elisabeth opened the door again for Peter-Bátschi, but instead of saying anything to her, he grumbled under his breath as he left, a hint of alcohol following him out.

"Next," Omama said to Elisabeth, "take your siblings to my house after mass. You can celebrate with our family today. Your mother needs rest." Omama helped herself to a slice of cheese from the table. "And happy Easter," she said before disappearing into the front room and closing the door behind her.

Elisabeth jumped back into her chair and drilled her gaze into each of her siblings.

"I know we're all thinking the same thing," she whispered.

"How long is she staying?" Luki asked, his eyes wide with fear.

"I don't know. But if each of you behaves well so long as she's here, I'll bake you delicious cookies once she's left."

Luki crossed his arms. "Are you going to hit me if I'm not good?"

Elisabeth promised herself to again ask Jesus for forgiveness. She had asked it last night and this morning upon waking, but it hadn't made her feel any better about having hit her brother. Perhaps asking during Easter mass today would help and then she could bury the memory in the back of her mind and forget it for the rest of her life.

"I'm so sorry, Luki," she said. "I promise I won't hit you. Yesterday was...very painful in many ways for all of us. But now things will be different, I promise. Do we have a deal?"

All three children nodded.

CHAPTER THREE

uliana stared at her homework question: "What experiences have you had that help you understand the events described in this book?"

"At least we got to pick our own book," she mumbled to herself. She'd chosen *From Anna*, by Jean Little, about a nine-year-old girl who had moved from Germany to Canada and who also discovered that she was visually impaired. *Sort of like me and Sophie put together, but younger,* she thought. She'd found the book at Aunt Anne's last week when she was over helping Sophie with her math homework. The book was young for Juliana, but once she explained her reasoning to Ms. Lee, her English teacher, she got permission to use it.

Juliana reviewed the paragraph she had just written, hoping to find an idea for what to write next:

Anna had difficulty with English, which of course wasn't a problem for me. But when I got here, normal things had different names. In Calgary, we called our composting program the green cart. In Kitchener, it's called the green bin. And in Calgary, we just called our city Calgary. In Kitchener, sometimes people talk about Kitchener, sometimes K-W, and sometimes Waterloo Region. I felt stupid sometimes at first because I didn't want to ask what the difference was.

"Maybe I should delete that last line," Juliana said to herself but decided against it. Miss Denise, her dance teacher, had said once that to be a good dancer, you had to be honest about your feelings. "I think Elisabeth was honest with her feelings in her sketchbook. I guess it's the same with writing."

She considered the question again. What other experiences of the past few months had helped her understand the events in the book? She fiddled with her hair as she tried to come up with an answer.

Streets!

She wrote some more:

I didn't go out much when I first got here, partly because I don't like the winter here—it's a different kind of cold— but also because the streets made no sense to me. In Calgary, most streets are numbered and most of our city is in a grid. So if someone's address is 11123 19 Ave. SE, you can look at street signs wherever you are in the city, and within 30 seconds, know where you have to go to get there. You can't do that here. That also makes me feel stupid, because I don't know where I am unless I look at my phone. I think that when Anna and her family moved to Canada, she felt disoriented, too.

But *From Anna* wasn't just about the awkwardness of moving to a new place. Anna had been teased and even bullied by her siblings and mother. Did anyone bully Sophie? Her family seemed pretty okay with her condition, though Rebecca, Sophie's twenty-three-year-old sister, was sometimes mean to Sophie. Aunt Anne certainly didn't bully her daughter.

Juliana wrote more:

I also picked the book because of my cousin, Sophie. Her mother's my mom's sister. When I first moved here, I thought she was blind, but I learned she was losing her eyesight. It's a disease called Stargardt disease. She can't read normal books anymore, but she can see the outline of my face if I'm close enough. But not if I'm standing far away. I help her with her math, and she helps me get to know my family. We have a lot of fun together and we sometimes go to a café in the neighbourhood together.

Juliana giggled as she remembered the two of them opening the door to Opa's cellar the first time they began searching for a funny photo of Mom from her childhood.

We both hate bugs, and the last time I was in my grandfather's cellar was at Christmas, when I found a special book. It was really gross in there. Sophie tricked me into going in there myself a few weeks ago and then the power went out! I shrieked!

But an uncomfortable memory also surfaced in Juliana: Without being able to see directly in front of her, Sophie sometimes knocked things over or dropped them and broke them. When Sophie dropped an old encyclopedia and the spine cracked, Juliana felt so sorry for her cousin. The accident soon turned into an amazing surprise, but Sophie had still been heartbroken at letting the book fall.

"Maybe I didn't pick the right story for my project," Juliana said aloud. *Nothing in my life compares to losing your eyesight. But the way Anna and her class tackled making those baskets in the book...I kind of felt like Sophie and I were working on a big mystery: where was that photo of Mom?* The memory made her smile for a moment, but when she looked at her clock, her happiness deflated. She'd been at this for almost an hour already.

"Can time pass any slower? I've only written a page so far." She reviewed the question again and tapped her cheeks in an effort to wake herself up. "Focus, Jules. You promised Mom you'd study. You still have to do that today." But her brain was empty. Not a single idea.

She reminded herself that this was not due for another couple of days, and that Opa and Mom were at the doctor's. That meant Juliana could dance in private for a little. Lately, Opa had begun watching her, and sometimes she didn't mind—he'd at least learned not to speak while she practised—but she wanted to dance alone today. She was still bummed about her marks and needed to get that sad energy out, something she preferred to do without an audience.

"Before I end up like a cracked egg," she said to herself. "And I'll at least practise my dances for tomorrow. I know that's not really studying, but it's for school, so it sort of counts."

Tomorrow was Juliana's first show with the school dance club at an old-age home. The glee club would be joining them, too. She was looking forward to performing without worrying about competition for once. She changed into some dance clothes, grabbed her bag, and headed into the basement.

Juliana didn't expect to get this nervous before a community show. The school bus with the dance and glee clubs pulled up to the main entrance of the old-age home. Ms. Lee stood up at the front of the bus and turned to face the students.

"Can I have everyone's attention?" she said. She needed to repeat herself a few times before the thirty or so students in the bus quieted down. "Thank you. We're about to go inside. Remember to use the hand sanitizer at the entrance and be friendly, but I know you all will be."

Why would Ms. Lee tell them to be friendly? Old people were usually nice.

Ms. Lee asked the bus driver to open the door, and everyone filed out. Costumes were simple and already on: jeans of any style and yellow t-shirts with "Dance" on the front for the dance club and "Glee" for the glee club. "Eby Heights" was written on the back in block letters along with the school's logo. Long hair in a ponytail, short hair neatly combed. Juliana usually needed at least an hour to get ready for competition dances. For this show, she'd only taken fifteen minutes.

The students filed out, and Juliana stayed close to a few girls she had gotten to know and who'd helped her learn the numbers. Two of them danced at another studio, and the third took dance at a music school in town. But everyone was friendly to everyone else, not mean like on some of the dance shows on TV.

The inside of the home looked pleasantly old-fashioned: deep reds, pine wood, floral wallpaper borders everywhere, with vases of artificial flowers placed on every available surface. Tables had been pushed off to one side and chairs spread out for a small audience. A few women were sitting in a corner, their white, permed hair perfectly coiffed, chatting. Juliana smiled at how cute they looked. A few men, their heads almost devoid of any hair, pulled some chairs up and began what appeared to be a lively debate. *So, Opa's not the only man who gets into heated discussions*, she thought, smiling. She couldn't wait to tell Sophie that—she'd get a good laugh out of it, too.

Juliana followed the group into a room where they dropped their belongings and began to warm up. They would start in about a half hour. Juliana's heart pounded with excitement.

THE GLEE CLUB MOVED IN UNISON AS THEY SANG "Somewhere Over the Rainbow," their faces full of joy and hope. But Juliana felt neither. Now finished her two dances, she sat off to the side and watched the rest of the show. Instead of enjoying the glee club's number, though, her gaze remained glued on the audience. The seniors who had been socializing when the students had first arrived were not the only ones in the audience anymore. More residents had been wheeled out right before the show: a woman with matted, white hair who talked to herself; a woman who looked asleep and whose thinning hair exposed most of her scalp; a man whose hands were clenched around washcloths. Some seniors even sat in wheelchairs that looked more like armchairs with wheels than the usual wheelchairs Juliana knew. All of these new people hardly moved their arms nor did they have any expression on their faces. In fact, if anything moved, it was usually only their eyes. Their hands looked jagged, as though their skin had been vacuum-sealed to their bones. The faint smell of urine hung in the air now, too.

"Where's Bertram?" a woman shouted from the audience to no one in particular. "Bertram! Where are you? You're missing the show!" An attendant gently touched her arm to calm her down. Juliana scanned the audience for anyone answering to Bertram but no one moved. She guessed Bertram wasn't there.

"No, Bertram has to hear about this! He loves hearing the little children sing!" The woman tried to get up. Juliana guessed from the thinness of her legs that this woman didn't walk anymore, though.

"Oh, stop it," another woman said in annoyance. "He's dead."

The attendant for the first woman rushed to stand

between them and asked her something. The woman nodded, and a moment later the attendant wheeled her elsewhere. The glee club members kept singing joyfully despite the disturbance, as Juliana expected. Dancers followed the same rule: the show must always go on unless the building's about to collapse.

As Juliana's eyes followed the woman, she noticed a group of happy men. One leaned over to another and whispered something. The second man smiled kindly and nodded. He reminded Juliana of Opa and the smile that lit up his face whenever she asked about Elisabeth.

Behind the men, though, sat a man in one of those big wheelchairs. He appeared frozen: his mouth hung open, his eyes stared at nothing, and his head hung a little to the side. He wore a bib that had wet spots on it.

Juliana swallowed to keep her stomach contents down. *Where were all these people when we arrived?*

During her dances, Juliana had fought to stay focused. Shoutouts of encouragement from her teammates at competitions and lots of cheering during year-end shows didn't bother Juliana. On the contrary, they helped her dance better. But random conversations or unexpected cries or unpleasant smells...she had never danced with those kinds of distractions before.

A woman from the audience shouted and Juliana jumped, jolted out of her thoughts.

Ms. Lee sat down next to her and whispered, "Are you okay? I saw how that woman startled you."

Juliana nodded, though it was a flat-out lie.

"Are you sure? I've been watching you for the past ten minutes, Juliana, and you've gone from scared to terrified and back again. You don't look okay."

"I'm fine," Juliana said, unable to pull her gaze from the small audience. The questions in her head wouldn't stop: Was this Opa's future? Was this the real reason she and her parents had moved here? To make sure he wouldn't end up like this? Or was he going to, anyway?

Oh my god, Juliana thought, trying to not let on to Ms. Lee that she'd realized something. *Rachel and I said back in Calgary that Mom's family should've put Opa in a home instead of making us move halfway across the country.* Her stomach turned into knots. Any ads for retirement homes she had ever seen, whether at bus stops or at the mall, always showed old people smiling and enjoying an activity, like reading a book with a grandchild or walking hand-in-hand with their spouse outdoors. They never showed people so... Juliana didn't want to let the word form in her mind. It was mean but she couldn't prevent it. *They never showed people so gross.* The wet spots on that man's bib were probably drool.

"Juliana, look at me."

Juliana turned her head and Ms. Lee's gentle face greeted her. "Are you sure you're all right? I know this isn't competition dance. You're probably used to a higher standard…"

Was that what Ms. Lee thought? That the dancing was so bad it embarrassed Juliana to participate? She needed to correct that right away, but how? Juliana couldn't admit to her teacher what she and Rachel had said in Calgary.

I even said the same thing to Mom in the car on the trip here, she realized. Her stomach began to churn.

"Juliana?"

"No, really, Ms. Lee," she whispered back. "I guess I just feel bad for those people." She tried to smile a little and relax her shoulders, but Ms. Lee still looked suspicious. "I'm really okay, Ms. Lee. This is a good experience for me."

Ms. Lee began to move away. "I need to help with the last dance. Talk to me if you need to, understood?"

Juliana nodded, and after Ms. Lee returned to the dressing room, Juliana's gaze returned to the man at the back with the bib.

Juliana had fought tooth and nail against moving to Kitchener, but she had acknowledged to Mom just last month that she was happy they'd moved. Juliana had met extended family—including Sophie—and she enjoyed spending time with them. She missed her best friend, Rachel, but they'd found a new normal for their long-distance friendship, and Juliana had fun with her new friends—Jasmine at the studio, and Meghan and Shawna at school. With time, her circle of friends would grow. Of course, nothing surpassed discovering Elisabeth's sketchbook and chatting with Opa to learn more about his mother.

But none of those reasons had anything to do with helping Opa.

They're all reasons that benefit me, she thought.

Opa had just turned seventy-one. Was he now one year closer to ending up like that man because of his Alzheimer's?

CHAPTER FOUR

"How is Lissa-Néni?" Georg asked in a low voice.

Elisabeth glanced around to make sure no one else in the church yard was listening. Georg, his wife, Eva, and his friend, Stefan, all stepped in a little closer so she could speak softly.

"I didn't hear her at night, so I think she slept through." Elisabeth didn't tell them about the rolled-up sheets. The way Margarethe-Néni had taken them from her told her it was something private. "And she insisted that I bring the children to Easter mass."

Out of the corner of her eye, Elisabeth caught Eva rubbing her belly. She and Georg were expecting their first baby, though it was Georg's second. His first wife and child had died of a fever while he fought in the war. Elisabeth prayed to Jesus that Eva would deliver a healthy child.

Georg was Margarethe-Néni and Konrad-Bátschi's oldest son and therefore heir to his family's home and blacksmithing workshop. The war, now over for almost two years, had left Georg a shell of his former self. He spoke very little and often became lost in nightmares and staring spells. Elisabeth had come to accept this about her cousin, but most of their congregation ridiculed him whenever the chance arose.

"How are you doing?" Stefan asked. "This can't be easy on you." Stefan's one year at war, where he had lost most of one arm, had been followed by two years in captivity in Russia. Elisabeth believed Stefan had nightmares in his sleep, but he didn't suffer the same fits and spells that Georg did.

She shrugged. "I have to push through and keep my family together, as Georg told me yesterday."

Eva touched Elisabeth's shoulder. "You know you can talk to us if you need help. I'm sure Maria will help you, too."

Haibach Maria was Elisabeth's best friend. She had come over to the Schuhmacher household on many occasions to help, usually without being asked.

Elisabeth nodded, acknowledging Eva's suggestions.

Another voice intruded on their conversation. "Elisabeth, how are you doing? How is your father?"

Elisabeth took a deep breath as she turned around. She recognized the voice of the church gossip: Herr Meier.

Out of politeness, the four of them opened their tight circle to admit him. Herr Meier did not hide his up-and-down inspection of Georg. He followed that with a look of pity for Eva, and said hello to Stefan. Stefan barely nodded back.

"I'm doing well, Herr Meier, thank you, and so is Tata."

"And your mother? I'd like to give her my regards, of course, but I can't find her today."

Elisabeth bristled, but she had to say something. Otherwise, he might pry further. "She's fallen ill, unfortunately."

Herr Meier's mouth turned upside down in an attempt at feigning sadness. "What ails her?"

"Her stomach isn't well." It wasn't exactly a lie, but Jesus would understand that Mammi didn't want Herr Meier to know everything, wouldn't He? After all, there was a slight chance that Frau Molnár hadn't told everyone yet. She was at the house right now and had left the Schuhmacher house last night. Surely her gossip didn't travel *that* fast.

Herr Meier, his chin in the air, looked around the church yard. "A stomach illness that has also kept your good Omama, Schuhmacher Margarete, and the midwife away from Easter mass?"

Georg stepped in. "Her stomach isn't well, Herr Meier."

Herr Meier looked up at Georg and took a step back. "Don't touch me."

Georg's large build made many people nervous. Before the war, the wrong word with Georg could land a man on the losing end of a fight. Now, they feared his fits, where he sometimes unknowingly lashed out at anyone who tried to stop them. Konrad-Bátschi had suffered several bruises in trying to stop his son from behaving as he did. According to Stefan, Georg's fits had begun during the war. Elisabeth was one of few people in their church congregation—and likely in their village—who accepted that these fits were not Georg's fault. Sadly, even Georg believed he deserved them.

Herr Meier adjusted his hat. "I'm speaking to Elisabeth, not you, Georg. In fact, you should do your cousin a favour and step out of her life. She's old enough now to find a husband, and no one will marry her with you around."

Herr Meier's comments made Elisabeth's blood boil. She fought to push her anger down, knowing it might get her in trouble and embarrass Mammi and the rest of her family. Elisabeth needed to act as ladylike as possible now.

"Who Elisabeth marries is none of your concern," Stefan added with a quick glance at Elisabeth. Did he blush? *No,* Elisabeth thought. *He must be as angry as me.*

"I'm only inquiring after Frau Schuhmacher's health, like a good Christian. I'd like to know what I can ask Jesus for."

You can ask Him to give you a reason to leave this village, Elisabeth thought and then asked Jesus for forgiveness.

"That Frau Schuhmacher gets well," Georg replied.

"Herr Meier! Is Georg bothering you again?"

Elisabeth closed her eyes in frustration. Why was Jesus doing this to her? She tried to smile at her uncle as he approached the group. Peter-Bátschi gave her a polite nod, but his gaze remained fixed on Georg.

Herr Meier raised his voice. "He interrupted me and wouldn't allow me to finish my conversation with Elisabeth."

Elisabeth's anger burst out of her. "He did not interrupt you!"

"And now he's making his cousin lie," Herr Meier continued.

"No, he isn't!" Elisabeth shouted back.

Heads turned and Elisabeth's cheeks grew hot.

Georg showed no signs of annoyance on his face. "It's all right," he said, his voice low as usual. "This is not new."

"It is to me, because he's accusing me of lying, too."

"Not at all, Elisabeth," Herr Meier said, his tone cool. "Do you see, Herr Braun?" Herr Meier said to Peter-Bátschi. "Look at how Georg is making your niece behave. This is highly improper for a young woman her age."

Peter-Bátschi added, "This isn't the first time, either."

Peter-Bátschi was referring to the time when Georg believed someone had launched a bomb. He had pulled Elisabeth and Stefan down to the muddy ground to protect them, but the bomb turned out to be nothing more than a child's ball. Peter-Bátschi, along with others in the crowd, had wasted no time in ridiculing Georg. He then warned Elisabeth to stay away from her cousin, because people might refuse to bring their shoes and boots to Mammi for repair.

"Leave him," Peter-Bátschi told Elisabeth now. "I'm sure your mother would prefer that you speak with *respectable* people. Or do you want to cause her more distress?"

A nod from Georg told Elisabeth to follow her uncle. Not wanting to cause more of a scene, she said, "I suppose I should say hello to Little Sophie and Sophie-Néni, too, before mass." She followed her uncle to his family. The look of satisfaction on Herr Meier's face made her wish she'd slapped him today instead of Luki yesterday.

Now a *groβmädchen*, a confirmed girl, Elisabeth sat at the front of the church with the other confirmed girls and boys. As much as she had tried to enjoy mass, the hundreds of eyes staring at her made her uncomfortable. She barely rejoiced in Jesus's resurrection and only remembered at the very end to ask Him for forgiveness for hitting Luki yesterday. She was certain everyone was wondering what had happened to Mammi. *Or were they staring at me because I'd lost my patience outside?*

As soon as mass finished, she collected her siblings as

they came down from the balcony, where all children sat, and instructed them to follow Peter-Bátschi and Sophie-Néni to their house. Elisabeth rushed home before anyone asked her about Mammi or said anything else. Her uncle's behaviour had even embarrassed her too much to say anything to Georg, Eva, or Stefan.

She entered her family's front gate, walked through the front yard, then the second gate into the poultry yard, and up to the house door at the side of their white, thatch-roofed, three-room home.

Elisabeth found Mammi sitting at the kitchen table still dressed in her nightgown, her face pale, and her hair hanging all the way down her back. The midwife was gone but Omama and Margarethe-Néni sat with Mammi, each drinking—Elisabeth took a whiff—coffee? The Schuhmachers hadn't had coffee in the house for several years now because of the war, but Elisabeth remembered when she was Luki's age how Mammi would make coffee every morning before her day began. The familiar smell comforted Elisabeth.

Unfortunately, despite drinking something she enjoyed, Mammi's face turned into a scowl. "You're to be at your uncle's."

"But I just wanted to see how you were doing…" Elisabeth replied, not understanding why Mammi wouldn't be happy that her eldest daughter had come to check on her.

"You've again disobeyed your elders. All of us, in fact.

You were told to stay with your siblings and take them to Peter's."

Elisabeth's jaw dropped. "But..." The Christian thing to do was to see if her mother needed help. Why was Mammi angry? Elisabeth remembered Georg's warning about Mammi's temper, though, and thought that maybe Mammi's anger kept her from acting like a Christian herself right now.

"I'm fine," Mammi said, her voice sharp. "Now, go."

"But..."

Omama stood up and hobbled over to Elisabeth. "I'll come with you a little ways," she said. Usually an unpleasant woman, Omama was strangely gentle with Elisabeth this time.

"No, it's all right," Elisabeth said, feeling dejected despite Omama's rare moment of kindness. "Thank you."

But Omama slipped out of her house shoes and into her outdoor leather slippers and followed Elisabeth to the road.

"What your *mammi* is going through is not for young eyes," she said. "Even though you are now a woman in our church, your body has not become that of a woman yet. There are some things you cannot know about until you are ready."

Elisabeth's body had not become a woman's yet? She knew that her chest would grow, but what else would happen to her? She would read about it later in Tata's encyclopedia when she had a private moment. Given that the topic was a woman's body, it was certainly something neither Mammi nor her siblings could catch her doing. *But with Omama in the house now, I may have to wait until she leaves.* Omama didn't approve of Elisabeth reading. She often said Elisabeth should put her time to better use.

"While I'm here, though," Omama continued, "I'm going to take care of the household. One thing I've told Lissa already is that I dislike how little you've done to find a husband."

"But Omama, I was just confirmed last week!" Elisabeth said. Although Mammi and Omama had tried introducing Elisabeth to a boy earlier this year, a serious search could not begin until after a girl was confirmed.

"You don't have to wait for confirmation to invite families over or spend more time visiting neighbours and friends so mothers and matchmakers can get to know you better."

It had indeed been a long time since Elisabeth had visited her friends in the evening. This tradition had a name: *majen.* Girls would invite their friends over to gossip and work on their handicrafts. Sometimes a mother or even a grandmother—someone respected by everyone for a specific handicraft, like knitting or embroidery—would teach the girls as they talked. Elisabeth enjoyed many handicrafts, but she was happy to not have to listen to gossip these past few months.

"Lissika," Omama continued, "I needn't remind you that the war has left fewer men to marry these days. Do want to be forced to marry someone who's as old as your father or who lives in another village?"

Elisabeth shivered at the thought. Such marriages did occur but to marry a man at least twenty years her senior frightened her. It meant that when she was thirty, he would be fifty. When she was forty, with a brood of children at home, he would be sixty and, God willing, still alive. To live in another village? She'd be so far away from her family. The wife always moved in with the husband, of course. She didn't know where the next Lutheran German congregation was: the Germans in all the villages around Semlak were Catholic. There was a Calvinist German church in Semlak, and a few Germans attended the local Catholic church, but to find a husband at either of those was out of the question.

You won't do that to me, Jesus? Elisabeth asked. *You'll help me find someone here, in my church and village, won't You?*

Omama interrupted Elisabeth's thoughts. "We also need to make sure the crops are properly planted. Rosina can help me during the day and Anna can help me when she gets home from school. Beginning Tuesday, you will go to the *salasch* each day to make sure crops are planted properly—I don't trust Georg with your family's land. Tomorrow you will show me where everything here is so I can take care of the household."

A *salasch* was farmland with a homestead that lay outside the village. Opa Schuhmacher—Tata's father—had owned it, and when he passed away, he had left most of the land to Konrad-Bátschi, Georg's father. Tata had inherited a strip of land that could feed a family, but no more. Between Mammi, Tata, and Elisabeth, with some help from the three younger siblings, they could tend to their land, and Tata's shoemaking business helped pay for extra labour when it was needed. However, without Tata at home, managing the seven acres was next to impossible. Mammi was slower at shoemaking than Tata, so where Tata took a day or two off as needed, Mammi did not. That left Elisabeth in charge of the fields as well as everything else in the household.

It was a gift from God that Georg and his brother Samuel had stepped in to help this year. However, the only ones who approved of the arrangement were Georg and Eva, Samuel and Deaf-Lissi, Elisabeth and her siblings, and, begrudgingly, Mammi. Omama disapproved strongly of it, as did Konrad-Bátschi and Margarethe-Néni.

"And you *must* visit my family this week," Omama continued. "Little Sophie is inviting friends and family over one evening. You *must* get out more often."

As much as Elisabeth did not like gossiping, she did miss spending time with others her age. With Omama tending to the household, Elisabeth could spend her time on the *salasch* without worrying about an additional list of chores at home and instead enjoying time with some of her father's family. Since she had promised her siblings special cookies if they behaved all week with Omama, she knew they would be fine with this arrangement, too.

Elisabeth stepped onto the road, and Omama closed the gate behind her.

Omama continued. "We also need to make sure you're ready for next Sunday's dance. It would be embarrassing if you had no one to dance with at your first one, wouldn't it?"

Next Sunday's dance? All the whirling skirts and loud stomps on the dance floor! The live band playing slow waltzes and energetic polkas! Elisabeth hadn't let herself think about the dances until now, because it would've seemed disrespectful to Jesus during Lent. After Mammi's miscarriage yesterday, she hadn't thought of it. Now that Omama brought it up, Elisabeth felt giddy. She smiled and nodded, and although Omama barely smiled—like Mammi, she believed smiling made her look stupid—she looked satisfied.

Maybe having Omama here to help for the week wouldn't be so horrible after all. Elisabeth headed for Peter-Bátschi's house, her mind changed about Omama's stay.

CHAPTER FIVE

Juliana wiped the sweat off her brow as she exited the studio with the rest of her ballet class. Today of all days their ballet teacher had chosen to focus on adage—all the slow work—in class instead of allegro—the big jumps and movements. Juliana craved something faster to expel her pent-up emotions before Mom picked her up. Juliana hadn't talked to anyone about her dance club's show, and if she didn't say something to someone, she was going to crack wide open.

"Can I ask you something?" Juliana said to Jasmine. With Jasmine's parents being a police officer and a nurse, maybe she could help make Juliana feel better. Besides, Jasmine had talked to Juliana before about dementia, so she should understand what Juliana was going through.

"Yeah, shoot," Jasmine answered.

But now that Juliana had Jasmine's attention, her thoughts froze. "Listen...I...um..." Should Juliana start about the man at the home? Or ask about how Opa's Alzheimer's would progress? Or maybe ask about Jasmine's day at school and ease in to asking about the man at the home? Or Opa's Alzheimer's?

They entered the intermediate girls' change room.

Jasmine checked her phone. "I've got a lot to study tonight, so I can't talk long. My science teacher likes giving us a test every two weeks."

"Ugh, mine's like that," Juliana said, relieved at the ice breaker.

"Dad's already outside waiting for me, so I need to get going. What's up?"

Juliana's thoughts jumbled in her head like the energy in her body. She blurted out, "I saw something today that really upset me."

A few heads in the change room turned, and Juliana regretted raising the topic.

But if I get into the car upset, Mom's going to guess something's up. I have to talk to someone about this, she thought. She had managed to stay quiet on the way to the studio, convincing herself ballet would focus on allegro tonight. No such luck on the drive home.

Jasmine slid her shoes off and threw them in her bag. "Okay."

Jasmine's voice, though, suggested to Juliana she wasn't

fully paying attention. Should she drop the topic? *Jules, you've got five minutes to get over this before Mom picks you up,* she reminded herself.

"I did that show at the old-age home I told you about."

"Mmhmm..." Jasmine slipped on a pair of workout pants.

"And, well, it kind of freaked me out."

Jasmine raised an eyebrow at Juliana. "How?"

The others in the room now watched Juliana, interested in the answer to Jasmine's question. Juliana's cheeks burned. This was not a good idea, but now she had to follow through.

"Well, just the way old people, you know, how they act when, like, things don't..." What words described what she was thinking? Juliana didn't want her dance teammates to think she was mean.

"Lots of dementia patients?" Jasmine asked.

"I guess so, yeah. Is that how Opa will end up? Immobile in a wheelchair, wearing a bib to catch his drool?"

A few of the girls wrinkled their noses.

But Jasmine didn't. She threw a sweatshirt over her head as casually as if Juliana had said it was raining outside. "It is what it is. Nothing you can change. Just accept that that's what the end of life looks like for some people."

Mackenzie, another dancer on their team, said, "Those homes are so gross. I can't go inside them."

The insensitivity of the comment caught Juliana off guard, leaving her speechless. At the same time, she'd also thought it was gross, which made her feel guilty now, too.

"Listen, I need to go," Jasmine said. "Is there anything else you wanted to talk about?"

That was it? That was Jasmine's advice? To accept that Opa would end up like a baby in a grown man's body? Rachel would've listened and tried to comfort her somehow, even if she thought Juliana was wrong.

"Well, yeah, I mean, what I saw really scared me. Your parents deal with old people. I thought you might, I don't know, be able to help me here."

"Juliana, my dad has seen people murdered before his eyes, has shot criminals himself, and so, so much more. One officer he often worked with even committed suicide because of the stress. Mom has seen doctors take comatose patients off life support. I get that watching someone you love wither away is scary, but your grandfather is fine as far as you've told me. Or has something changed?"

"Um, no, I guess not." Now Juliana felt bad for feeling the way she felt. *I guess there are worse things out there.*

"Okay, well, good to hear. I should get going. See you tomorrow." Jasmine lifted the strap of her dance bag over her head, setting it on the opposite shoulder, and grabbed the door handle.

"Yeah, I mean, no! Jasmine, I was really freaking out there. I almost threw up. I swear I could even smell pee."

Now everyone in the room wrinkled their nose in disgust.

Jasmine shrugged. "Some wear briefs—adult diapers, in case you don't know what those are."

Several now repeated, "Diapers?" and giggled.

Juliana's jaw dropped.

Jasmine's gaze swept past each girl in the change room as she spoke. "You should only hope no one laughs at you if illness or bad genes leave you like that." Everyone's faces straightened out and Jasmine turned her attention back to Juliana. "Getting old is complicated and not always pretty. But they're still people and not everyone's life ends the same way. Forget whatever you saw and just move on. I've gotta go."

Juliana rushed to get her stuff together so she could follow Jasmine out. She ran up behind her.

"But they looked so neglected," she said. "I mean, who lets that happen to them?"

Jasmine slipped into her runners and Juliana did the same. "No one 'lets' that happen. At least not in most cases, and I'm certain your parents won't let that happen to your grandfather." She stopped for a moment to look at Juliana. "It's great that you care so much about your grandfather. But Alzheimer's will change him. Do what I've said before and spend as much time with him as you can. You do kind of live in a bubble: there's a lot worse out there. Happy studying."

I live in a bubble? Juliana thought as Jasmine climbed into her father's car. *Your parents chose their careers. My grandfather did not choose his Alzheimer's.*

A short car horn told Juliana that Mom had already arrived. *Great. Now I feel worse than I did before.* She did her best to paste on a smile and pretend like she was about to perform the happiest jazz number in the whole world. Hopefully she could fool Mom a second time.

"MADE IT," JULIANA WHISPERED TO HERSELF. SHE THREW HER dance bag on her bed and dropped next to it. Mom had asked about Juliana's strange behaviour, but Juliana had continued to smile, said she'd finished her homework for the day, and had even studied.

She had only studied about ten minutes, but she had studied nonetheless and Mom seemed satisfied with her answer. Good enough, right?

It was now close to ten o'clock, so Juliana wasn't about to open her books. She unpacked her dance shoes, placed them side by side on the floor, and dusted them with baking soda she kept in a saltshaker on her dresser. Baking soda kept her shoes—and therefore her dance bag—from smelling like stinky feet. She'd kept up the habit faithfully in Calgary and wanted to get back into it. Aside from making her shoes and dance bag smell better, Juliana hoped it would help her feel like life here was almost like it was in Calgary, and then she could study like she used to, too.

As she dusted her pointe shoes, her phone rang: Dad.

"Hey, sweetheart."

"Hey."

"I'm sorry I didn't call you after school today. I had to load the truck around the time I figured you were done with your show and I couldn't take a break."

In other words, he had to work. Same old, same old. "Yeah, sure, that's okay."

"But Mom said you were still awake, so here I am. How was the show?"

What should Juliana answer? If she told Dad the truth, he'd tell Mom. But her fear and sadness from earlier today mixed with anger from Jasmine's unhelpful advice and everyone's insensitive laughter. She wasn't going to sleep unless she let the energy out somehow, but she didn't want to spend an hour on the phone talking about it either.

"Okay," she said, her voice sounding flatter than she had hoped.

"Only okay? You were looking forward to the show. Was it too much in the end?"

Juliana didn't want Dad to think that she'd made the wrong decision. After all, she'd enjoyed the club's practices and all the other students were nice. *And it'll help me get better faster so I don't drag my team down as much anymore.*

Joining the dance club helped her out. Only today didn't go so well. No big deal, right?

"No. Everything went well. I'm just tired from dance, that's all."

"Jules, you don't sound particularly convincing."

Juliana set her dusted dance shoes aside. "No, really, Dad, I'm good. I did the show—the seniors liked it, and the others on the team are nice—then I came home and did my homework, even studied a little, and now I've finished three hours of dance. I'm just tired. And a good night's sleep makes studying easier the next day, right?"

Dad laughed. "Since when have you worried about a good night's sleep so you can study better? You used to stay up way past your bedtime to study."

Juliana slid her bag under her bed. *Shoot. Caught*, she thought. *But I don't want to talk to him about it.* In truth, talking about something like this on the phone was too awkward. The signal sometimes cut in and out, or Dad would ask her to wait a second while he called in a crazy driver. Some drivers even tailgated him, trying to take advantage of the drag from the truck to save on gas while remaining invisible to Dad. His stupid-driver stories were never-ending. Juliana understood Dad needed to report these drivers, but it made talking to him while he drove difficult.

"I'm just tired, Dad."

"Okay. Whatever's bothering you, I guess I'm not going

to get it out of you by calling at ten. Have a good sleep, and we'll talk when I get home. But you can always talk to your mom, too, eh? Or Aunt Anne if you need to. This is why we moved here. So you'd have family for once."

"Really, I'm fine."

"Okay. Good night, sweetheart."

"Good night, Dad. Drive safely."

"I will."

They hung up, and Juliana's stomach growled. "I guess I'll get a snack. I'm not falling asleep anytime soon, anyway."

She walked down the hallway and startled: Opa was sitting in the kitchen reading the newspaper. She hadn't heard him coming up the stairs.

"Yulika!" he said, his smile wide. "Your mother heard you on the phone with your father, so she asked me to tell you she went to the grocery store. She forgot something." He laughed in spite of himself. "And they say I'm the one who forgets. How was your day?"

Suddenly Juliana's heart began to race in her chest, her palms began to sweat, and her thoughts focused on one need: to get out of the kitchen. Why was she reacting like this? *Or rather, why is my body?*

"Um, good, actually. My day was good, Opa. Thanks for telling me. I'm going to bed."

Opa nodded, his eyes glued to the paper. *"Gute nacht,"*

he said, which Juliana knew meant "good night" in German.

"Good night!"

She hurried back to her room and caught her reflection in the long mirror on her closet door. Her face was pale, even for skin as white as hers at the end of winter. She touched her forehead. Not hot. But her heart wouldn't stop racing and she struggled to catch her breath.

"What's happening to me?" she asked herself, but no answer came to her. She grabbed her phone and looked up her symptoms.

CHAPTER SIX

Inside the Braun household, the men shouted and laughed as they played skat in the front room while the older girls and women washed the dishes and cleaned up the back room, preparing it for the parade of desserts hiding out back in the cellar.

"Be careful!" Elisabeth called out to one of her young cousins. Some of the children were running through the small house, squealing as they chased one another. *If this were my family, I would send the children outside to run around. Something will get broken,* Elisabeth thought. But chaos reigned in this household.

"Lissika, pass me that serving dish," said Braun-Néni, one of Mammi's two sisters, as she completed her duty: scraping all extra food into the slop pail to feed to the pigs afterwards. Everyone had called her by the family name for as long as Elisabeth could remember because she had married last and everyone else had a Margarethe in their new family. Her actual name was Margarethe Schäfer. Elisabeth didn't believe Braun-Néni's husband was related to Stefan, but one could never be sure in such a small community, and one certainly did not ask.

Elisabeth passed her aunt a serving dish from the stack of dishes on the kitchen table and accepted a wet plate from Resi-Néni, Mammi's other sister, who stood at the end of the line of women, dipping dishes into a bowl of water to rinse off any remaining soap. Elisabeth dried the plate off and placed it on top of a small pile of similar plates. With the Easter celebrations so large, Mammi's two sisters had brought extra dishes, so it was important to separate them after drying.

Sophie-Néni, Peter-Bátschi's wife, came into the kitchen from outside, a bowl of fresh washing water in her hands. "How is Lissa?" she asked as she exchanged one of the washing bowls. "Does she need anything? Modr said she insisted we not come. Lissa can be as stubborn as a mule."

"And proud as a peacock," Resi-Néni added, her nose turned up. "Each time this has happened, she's never allowed us to help her. But Margarethe Schuhmacher is there right now."

Because she came even though Mammi didn't want her to, Elisabeth thought. At the same time, Margarethe-Néni completed many tasks faster than Omama, and if Elisabeth couldn't help because she wasn't a woman yet, who else would?

"That nosy woman can be worse than Meier Josef," Sophie-Néni said. "Why is she allowed in Lissa's home and her own family isn't?"

All the women stopped and turned their heads to face Elisabeth, whose words froze in her mind. Mammi had lost a baby, and all her sisters did was compare her to a mule and a peacock and then put Elisabeth on the spot with a question like that?

"Actually, my aunt is already gone," Elisabeth answered. "I just came from home. Mammi's tired, but she's doing better." Her response didn't answer her aunts' questions, but at least she had said something.

Michael, one of Resi-Néni's two children, chased his younger sister, Rosina, through the kitchen, startling Sophie-Néni, who almost dropped the bowl of dirty water she still carried in her hands.

"Michael! Rosina!" Resi-Néni shouted at her children as her sister-in-law stepped outside to dump out the bowl.

"I'm not doing anything wrong!" Elisabeth's sister yelled from the back room, where she was laying out fresh cloth napkins with Anna and Little Sophie.

"Not you!" Elisabeth shouted back at her. "Haibach Rosina!"

No relation to Maria, so far as Elisabeth knew.

Answering to the wrong person happened often in Semlak. Although many people had nicknames—like Samuel's wife, Deaf-Lissi, who wasn't actually deaf, and Little Sophie, who had just been confirmed with Elisabeth and was therefore clearly not little—not everyone did.

Sophie-Néni returned just as Little Sophie shouted through the house, "Did Lissa-Néni lose her baby? Is that why she didn't come to church today?"

The half-dry plate in Elisabeth's hands slipped and split into pieces on the dirt-and-chaff floor. Everyone froze: the men with their playing cards in hand and cigars or cigarettes hanging out of their mouths, the women with their dishes, and even the children who stopped running. Rosina and Anna stared at Elisabeth from the back room, unsure of what to do with this new information. Even Luki, who was playing with a cousin by the backside of the stove in the front room, looked questioningly at his oldest sister.

Without hesitation, Sophie-Néni marched over to her daughter and slapped her across the face. The unspoken rule in Elisabeth's household said that physical punishment stopped after confirmation unless someone behaved very poorly. *I guess that's one rule we have in common,* she thought. *Maybe the only one? How could Little Sophie not know that one didn't ask such questions?* Elisabeth still thought it wrong that Sophie-Néni hit her daughter. But at the same time, that's just how it was.

"I have told you more times than I can count that one

does *not* discuss a woman's curse in front of others!" Sophie-Néni reprimanded her daughter.

Little Sophie broke out into tears and pressed herself into a corner in the back room, trying to hide. Elisabeth felt her cousin's embarrassment and wanted to help. But was it better to ignore what had just happened, as one usually did? Elisabeth might insult her aunt and uncle if she tried to comfort her cousin. As Elisabeth picked up the pieces of the broken plate, she glanced at her aunt. There was not a sign of remorse on her face. On the contrary, and unsurprisingly, other women nodded at her decision to slap her daughter.

As the men returned to their card game, the children to their running, and the women and older girls to their washing, Elisabeth set the shards off to the side and looked up at Jesus who, like in all Christian households in Semlak, hung above one of the doorways in the kitchen. *You showed compassion, no matter the situation, didn't You?*

But before she could even take a step toward her cousin, her own siblings congregated around her.

"Shouldn't we go looking for the baby if it's lost?" asked Anna.

"But we don't have a baby," Rosina said.

"Because it belongs to another *mammi*," Luki said.

Although the women and older girls in the kitchen had returned to their duties, their side glances told Elisabeth they were listening to every word she would say.

"Go back to your chores and your play. The longer I'm idle, the longer dessert will be."

At the mention of dessert, her siblings jumped for joy and returned to their activities.

What would she tell Mammi? She would have to tell her something. The fourth commandment said to honour one's father and mother, and that meant telling them the truth. But although cake and cookies might keep her siblings happy, they would certainly not keep Mammi's anger away.

I only hope I don't get slapped, Elisabeth thought.

Back at home, Elisabeth sat at the back-room table, her sketchbook on her lap and pencil in her hand. She looked up from her drawing often to see how happy everyone was this Easter evening.

A grin on her face, Anna *titscht* the tip of her reddish-brown hard-boiled egg against Luki's to see whose would crack first. But when Luki's egg stayed smooth and Anna heard the familiar *crunch* as the tip of her egg caved in, her grin disappeared.

"I won!" Luki cried, jumping up and down.

"You got lucky," Anna said, pouting.

The tradition took Elisabeth's mind off the embarrassing situation at Peter-Bátschi's that afternoon.

Luki set off to challenge Mammi's egg, and Elisabeth was surprised by the light that shone in Mammi's eyes as she played with her son. Still seated on her bed, she wore an old—but clean!—dress and her hair was pulled back into a braid, her head covered by a *haube*. Had Elisabeth's aunt and grandmother helped Mammi that much? What if Georg was wrong and Mammi wouldn't be very angry with the loss of this child? Elisabeth hoped so.

The four Schuhmacher children had returned home about an hour before to find that Margarethe-Néni was already gone. Omama was now putting the final ingredients into a chicken soup she had simmering on the stove. Sophie-Néni had packed some leftovers for the Schuhmachers so they wouldn't have to cook today, which Elisabeth appreciated. On their walk home, Elisabeth had reminded her siblings to not tell Mammi about the lost baby.

"If you talk to her about babies or say anything about babies in the house, no cookies," she had said.

"But if something's lost," Anna had replied, "we should help find it. Especially a baby."

"No questions," Elisabeth had repeated. "Don't even use the word 'baby.' Let Jesus help find the baby instead, all right?"

Her siblings had agreed, but did Jesus approve of her using His name in this situation? Elisabeth had hoped He would understand.

"I won again!" Luki cried and sought out another opponent.

Omama came to Elisabeth in the back room, grunted at her drawing, and spoke. "Margarethe washed your mother's sheets. Lissa should not have asked you to do that. You are not yet married nor have you blossomed yet. That you knew she was going to have a baby was already too much for your innocent thoughts."

Blossomed? What did Omama mean? Elisabeth wanted to steal away and read from Tata's encyclopedia. But she would have to wait for a day when the house was empty. *That could be a while*, she thought.

"I hope you're not drawing anything about what happened."

Elisabeth's eyes opened wide. "No, of course not! Just an egg that's been cracked from *titschen*. I want to remember it so I have something happy to tell Tata about Easter when he comes home."

Omama grunted again, mumbled that Elisabeth's drawing was a waste of time, and hobbled out to the kitchen to check on the soup. Elisabeth enjoyed not having to take care of cooking for once, though she wouldn't have been upset if Omama had asked for help either. It was part of her regular duties, after all.

Elisabeth set her pencil down and walked through the kitchen to the front room to ask Mammi if she needed anything.

"What's that?" She pointed to the needlework in Mammi's hands. It looked like the satin upper of a woman's dress shoe.

"You can see very well what it is," Mammi said, pulling the needle through the fabric.

"It's a shoe," Anna said. "But who's it for?"

"None of your business," Mammi said.

"Can I do the other one?" Anna asked.

Mammi looked up. "What a silly question. You are nine—"

"Almost ten!"

"It makes no difference. You still have many years before your handiwork is good enough to sell."

Why did Mammi have to answer in such a way? Anna still had much to learn, but there were nicer ways to speak.

"I can knit squares for the shoes," Rosina added.

"Where do you get such nonsense?" Mammi asked. "Who wears knitted squares on their feet?"

"My slippers when I was little were knitted," Rosina said. "And no one wears sewed flowers!"

"Rosina!" Omama said from the kitchen. "You *do not* speak to your mother that way. If you speak like that again, you will kneel in the box of corn."

Rosina's eyes watered. Every household had a box of dried corn kernels used for punishing children, but Elisabeth refused to physically discipline her siblings. She didn't believe Jesus would approve. Even though she had asked

Jesus for forgiveness today at church for hitting Luki, that she had hit him at all still gnawed at her. How did adults do it?

I have to keep my family together, she thought. *Hitting won't help.*

"Listen," Elisabeth said to her siblings. "You're both still too young to earn money with sewing. But you'll be able to one day if you practise. Go get your handiwork now and you can practise next to Mammi."

Both sisters sulked as they obeyed Elisabeth. Omama waddled into the back room, pulled out the basket she used for her own work, and joined the family in the front room. Luki was building a house of cards with Tata's deck.

"Lissa, I shake my head at your shoes," Omama said to her daughter. "No Lutheran wears decorated shoes. That would draw unnecessary attention to a woman."

Keeping her eyes on her needlework, Mammi replied, "Modr, our women want nice shoes, and they will pay me extra for this."

Omama shook her head in disapproval. "What does Pastor Fröhlich say about this?"

"He is not a woman," Mammi replied. Elisabeth fought back a giggle.

"You know what I mean. Women do not embroider shoes to make them lovely."

"Then why do we embroider shawls and hand-kerchiefs?"

"Because we've always done so."

"We've also always had a man in the household until the war came."

Omama dropped her hands and glared at her daughter. "All the more reason to return to how life was. With the way you are speaking to me, I wonder if you should kneel in that corn."

Omama's threat drew Mammi's full attention. "Kneeling in corn would be much easier than what I've just gone through, especially without my husband here."

Elisabeth caught Anna's and Rosina's questioning looks and quickly pointed out errors in their handiwork to distract them.

Omama resumed her work. "One should not put money before the Lord. Fancy shoes are for rich people who waste their money and lose their way."

"As I said, we embroider our shawls and handkerchiefs. Why must shoes be any different?"

"Then I quote Proverbs, chapter thirteen, verse eleven: 'Wealth gotten by vanity shall be diminished: but he that gathereth by labour shall increase.'"

Mammi replied, "Sewing is not labour? Seamstresses earn money by sewing and mending clothing. That we do not wear clothing with holes is a sign of vanity. That unmarried women's skirts are colourful is a sign of vanity. Potters earn their money by forming clay and painting decorations on it, when these decorations are unnecessary and therefore also vanity."

"There is nothing useful about decorative shoes."

Mammi stopped and looked at Omama again. "There is if they help a young woman find a suitable husband."

Omama paused for a moment and seemed to think Mammi's argument through. She finally nodded. "I had not thought of that."

Were the shoes for Elisabeth? Maybe even for next Sunday? Elisabeth's insides danced with anticipation, but nothing on Mammi's face betrayed who the shoes were for.

CHAPTER SEVEN

School the following day had provided a good distraction for Juliana, and her heart seemed to have calmed down. Although she'd tried looking up her symptoms online last night, the more she read, the more she worried—brain disorders, cancer, appendicitis, rare genetic conditions—so she'd shut her phone off.

But back at home now, Opa and the face of the man from the home fused into one in her mind. It wasn't fair! Why would he have to end up like that? The image of the one man, frozen in time (or in his mind), unaware of his surroundings, his head cocked to one side for no reason Juliana could discern. Was he wearing a diaper, too? *A brief,* she corrected herself. And how old was he? Seventy-three? Seventy-four?

"But what if he was just paralyzed?" she asked herself.

"Maybe he was in a bad accident a long time ago. Or maybe he was born that way. Lots of people are born disabled." These thoughts comforted Juliana. Opa wasn't paralyzed, so he wouldn't end up frozen like that, right? Why hadn't she thought of this before?

Someone knocked on the door and Juliana touched her trackpad to wake up her computer.

Mom popped her head in. "How's your studying going?"

Luckily, Juliana still had an assignment open, although she hadn't worked on it for almost an hour. "Good."

"What are you studying?"

"Oh, um, English. We have to write an essay—"

"But that's homework, not studying."

Why was Mom being so picky? Schoolwork was schoolwork. Juliana needed to turn this conversation around fast. "Well, it is, because we have to review what we learned in class about learning how to reflect on a book."

To Juliana's relief, Mom bought her excuse. "I see. That sounds really interesting, actually. You'll have to tell me more over supper. Which, by the way, is in fifteen minutes. Don't be late." She smiled at Juliana, who promised she'd be punctual, and closed the door.

Her laptop screen now shining in her face, Juliana switched to her web browser. She wanted proof that this man in the home was paralyzed and not in the final stages of Alzheimer's.

"But if he's paralyzed, what is there to look up?" She tapped her fingers on the keyboard, which gave her the feeling of doing something. "What would I search? 'Symptoms of paralysis?' That seems pretty obvious." A moment later, she typed "causes of paralysis" into the search bar and in a split second, ten links appeared. As she scanned them, she realized the futility of this search. The causes ranged from accidents to genetic problems, none of which she could figure out with only an image of this man in her mind.

"Would #paralysis show me anything? Or would other friends know something?" A moment later, Juliana changed her mind. Her social media feeds could be filled with negativity from time to time, which she didn't need right now. And would Opa want to be discussed so publicly? Probably not. Juliana certainly hated when Mom discussed her with her friends on social media.

That left researching advanced symptoms of Alzheimer's. Juliana typed in her search and stared at the results returned to her. But did she want to read all this? What if the symptoms of advanced stages of Alzheimer's really were like the condition of that man? Jasmine had said that dementia wasn't pretty. Reading symptoms that matched the man's would confirm Opa's future for Juliana.

"I don't like looking ahead in Elisabeth's book," she said to herself. "Why would I want to in Opa's life?"

What if Juliana learned Alzheimer's did turn people

catatonic near the end of their life? Jasmine had said nothing could stop the decline of Alzheimer's, but also that it didn't have to end that way. So Opa might still be fine in a few years. *Maybe I'm needlessly worrying myself.*

"Something I'm already good at and certainly don't need to practise anymore."

She tapped her feet on the carpeted floor as she stared at the search engine results and her thoughts returned to her initial hopes: that the man was somehow already disabled and therefore not an image of Opa's future.

Unable to sit still, Juliana lay on her back on the floor, stretched one leg out, and extended the other into the air. She grabbed the ankle of the extended foot and pulled her straight leg toward her face. She still had thirty or forty centimetres to go, while most of the dancers on her team could already touch their leg to their nose. Every minute of practice counted.

There were lots of different types of disabilities—several kids at school couldn't walk or move much. Those kids would grow up, so this man probably couldn't move when he was a kid.

She switched legs.

"But if I learn what to expect, then I can plan ahead. That would make things easier in the long run, right?"

She continued stretching, wavering between learning more about Alzheimer's and convincing herself that the man she had seen didn't have it.

"Juliana! Supper! You're late!" Mom called from the kitchen.

"Already?" Juliana said to herself. She apologized to Mom and stood up, confirming on her phone that twenty minutes had indeed passed.

She threw her hands up in the air. "More than an hour of not studying," she said. Why couldn't she concentrate like she used to in Calgary?

"What if I dust my shoes again?" she asked herself. Would that give her the feeling of living in Calgary and bring back her concentration? In her heart, she knew the answer was no.

JULIANA WOKE UP THE NEXT MORNING WANTING TO KILL HER alarm: she had lain half the night awake in her bed debating whether she should read up on Opa's future or not. Her shower didn't energize her either. Once she was dressed, she stumbled into the kitchen, where Opa was eating a bowl of cereal and milk.

"*Guten morgen*, Yulika," he said, his voice cheery.

Juliana yawned and Opa wagged a finger at her. "You were up late studying, right?"

She nodded, because she couldn't come up with an excuse that lay closer to the truth. Her brain felt like it had been stuffed with pointe shoe toe protectors.

Mom rushed into the kitchen. "Good morning, Tata," she said.

"*Guten morgen*, Katy," he replied.

Within thirty seconds, Mom began crunching down on her cereal. Juliana still hadn't gotten herself a bowl.

"You okay, sweetie?" Mom asked, her mouth full.

Juliana nodded. How could Mom act so normal knowing what her dad's future held?

"She was up late studying," Opa reported.

"That's good to hear, but you look haggard, sweetie. I didn't mean for you to lose sleep over your marks. That won't do you any good, either. If anything, I'm glad you've found a healthier sleep schedule here."

Juliana nodded again. How could she get those toe protectors out of her head?

"You've only got twenty minutes, eh?" Mom asked, shovelling more cereal into her mouth. "You'd better hurry."

Three minutes later, Juliana dropped into a chair and began eating her cereal. Mom rushed to the washroom to finish getting ready.

"Is everything all right?" Opa asked. "You have no colour in your face. Are you getting sick?"

A question Juliana could answer honestly. "No. Just tired." She stared at her cereal. Why had all the little *o*s stopped moving, like the man in the old-age home?

Stop it, she told herself. *Now you're going overboard.* She stirred the cereal with her spoon to make it move.

Opa folded his newspaper together. "You are quiet," he said. "You usually talk more in the morning. Not like right now."

Before Juliana answered, Mom rushed back out.

"You haven't eaten even half your breakfast?" She ripped open her wallet and grabbed some money. "Here. Buy yourself lunch today. I'm glad you're studying, Jules, but not so late, okay?"

Juliana nodded, feeling guilty about the lie. *But I really couldn't come up with anything else!* she thought in her defense.

Opa watched Mom leave, and once she closed the door behind her, returned his attention to his granddaughter.

"Is Katy being too hard on you because of your report card?"

Still staring into her bowl, Juliana shook her head.

"Mammi finished school in grade six," he said about Elisabeth. "She didn't have to worry about marks at your age. She wanted me to try hard in school because she was jealous that she couldn't learn as much when she was young. Then I moved to Canada, and nothing I learned in the *heimat* mattered."

Juliana recognized the word *heimat*. It didn't exist in English, but it sort of meant where your heart lives. Calgary was Juliana's *heimat*, but Kitchener was now her home.

"Different culture, different language," Opa continued. "What good is Russian literature when the only job you can find is making tires?"

Russian literature? But Opa was from Romania. What did Russian literature have to do with anything? Juliana nodded, not sure how to react. His words suggested not worrying about marks all the time was okay, but his tone suggested a "but" was coming.

It came.

"But you live in this beautiful country. You need good marks for a good job." He carried his bowl to the dishwasher. Juliana continued to stare at her cereal. Once at the door to the basement, Opa said, "Yulika, young people also need their sleep. They say that a lot in the news. Sleep is very important."

Juliana nodded again.

"And you need to say more," he said. "I know I've said this before, but it's important, Yulika. Your *omama* sometimes spoke up too much, and it got her into trouble. But you don't speak up enough. That's also not healthy. Something is wrong and you should tell someone." Opa wished her a good day and disappeared into the basement without saying another word.

Juliana let out a sigh of both relief and further guilt. She was relieved that she was finally alone, but being reminded of Elisabeth's limited education and desire to keep learning made Juliana feel even guiltier because she wasn't studying like she'd promised to.

Her mood now in the gutter, she dragged her feet to her bedroom, got her backpack, and headed to school.

On her way, her mind kept circling from the man to Opa to Mom. She arrived to her English class two seconds before the bell, but throughout class, she swallowed more yawns than she cared to count. As Ms. Lee talked about reflective reading, Juliana's mind wouldn't let go of the man and the old-age home.

I can't do it, she realized. *I can't go into one of those homes again. I just can't.*

But that would mean quitting the dance club, and Juliana never quit. Even when she had twisted her ankle and broken her wrist a few years back after she'd slipped on stage, she had watched dance class from the sidelines. She envied that her teammates could keep dancing, but everyone supported her every day, and she pulled through.

Why can't I look at old, sick people but I got through my accident? she asked herself.

In truth, the answer didn't matter. To paraphrase Jasmine, it was what it was. As Ms. Lee continued on with class and the frozen man's body and face grew in detail in Juliana's mind, her heart raced again. She still didn't understand why, only that it wasn't good.

When the bell rang, Juliana waited until the last

students in her class had asked Ms. Lee their questions. When Juliana approached, Ms. Lee looked concerned.

"Is everything okay, Juliana? You looked uncharacteristically checked-out today. You didn't even check your phone."

Juliana stared at the floor. She could tell Ms. Lee everything right now and finally share her feelings with someone who would probably understand. *Unlike Jasmine.* But what if Ms. Lee pushed Juliana to stay in the dance club? Juliana didn't like saying no to teachers—her friends back in Calgary often teased her for it. *But I can't go into another one of those homes!* She had decided.

"I, um, I need to quit the dance club, Ms. Lee." Before her teacher said anything, Juliana added, "I thought I'd be able to handle it and school and my dance studio training, but I can't. I have to study." She lifted her gaze to find Ms. Lee's arms crossed and brow furrowed.

"That doesn't sound like you, Juliana," she said. "You love dance, and when you asked to join, you said it was because you didn't have enough to do, despite this semester already having started. Your teachers from Calgary wrote that you're a very conscientious and bright student who likes to keep busy. I'm worried about you."

Juliana twirled her hair around her finger. "I know, but I was wrong. I really shouldn't have joined. I'm really sorry. Everyone in the club is really nice. I...I...I think I've just taken on too much. My marks aren't as good as they used to be."

Students for the next period started streaming in. Ms. Lee quickly closed one binder on her desk and opened up another. Juliana wanted to jump up and down to get rid of her nerves, but she didn't want Ms. Lee wondering whether she'd had too much caffeine this morning or took drugs or something.

Ms. Lee nodded. "I'm sorry to see you go so soon, though," she said. "You're a lovely dancer to watch on stage, and I think you would've enjoyed performing with the team. But it's your choice."

"Maybe next year?" Juliana offered as an olive branch.

"See how your summer goes and we'll talk in September. But if you change your mind as soon as next week, you can always come back. Understood?"

Juliana nodded. "Thank you."

She rushed out the door and to her next class, but not without feeling worse about herself than before.

I'm not a quitter, she thought, *but I just quit.*

She was becoming a stranger to herself.

CHAPTER EIGHT

"No, Lissika, I said get the butter first," Omama complained to Elisabeth. "Cheese is for supper tonight."

"But the butter is already next to the bread." Elisabeth pointed to a spot on the kitchen shelf where the bread sat, covered by a tea towel.

"And it has gone bad," Omama replied. "Bring fresh butter and I'll throw this in the slop pail. Luki, have you fed the animals yet?"

"Anna and I do that after breakfast," Luki insisted.

"I can't help you yet," Anna said.

"You can. You just don't want to," Luki replied.

Elisabeth mouthed "cookies" to them as Omama raised one hand to signal that she would hit them both. Luki ran out of the house without saying another word. Elisabeth followed him out the door, running around the house to the cellar at the back, cheese in hand.

"There's nothing wrong with cheese for breakfast," she said to herself. Every morning, the Schuhmachers ate bread with butter and jam. They often drank tea, too, though her siblings preferred milk. But Omama had wanted Elisabeth to first scrub down the kitchen table, which wasn't clean enough for her, and then help Anna and Rosina with their hair, even though Anna helped Rosina now, and then ensure the children's shoes were polished, when Elisabeth always did that *after* school, in other words, last Friday. Besides, today was Easter Monday, a holiday.

She reached for a jar of plum jam but hesitated. What if Omama wanted apricot jam? "She'll send me back if I bring the wrong one. Did she tell me which one? But Rosina likes apricot on one day and plum the next. Was today apricot day? Or plum day?" She raised her gaze to the ceiling. "Jesus, please help me survive this!" Elisabeth grabbed a jar of each and some butter and rushed back around the house and to the kitchen. She couldn't remember when a morning had been this chaotic since January. After Tata had left, in November, everyone still followed their morning routine, even though they felt sad. After Mammi had told Elisabeth over Christmas that the household was hers to take care of so Mammi could make shoes, Elisabeth learned to manage everything on her own. Now, Omama was turning everything upside down.

Elisabeth placed both jars and the fresh butter on the table.

"What's this?" Omama said, not a hint of happiness in her voice. "*One* jam, Lissika. *One!* Take the apricot jam back. We do not need to have extra jars at the table. The Lord had a clean table at His Last Supper, and so must we."

Rosina pouted and opened her mouth to protest. But before she got a word out, Elisabeth whispered, "Cookies...!" and Rosina closed her mouth again.

"Bring some sausage," Omama said. "Your brother and sisters are too skinny."

Sausage? At breakfast during the week? Mammi wanted to save the meat for supper, when everyone was much hungrier. She said one slept better on a full stomach. The family only ate meat for breakfast when heavy work on the fields was planned.

Elisabeth rushed out again. She wanted everything in the house cleaned up and perfect in case any boys came by to spray her. Spraying was an Easter Monday tradition in Semlak: young relatives—boy cousins, usually—would visit family and spray the girls and women with a little perfume or rosewater. Elisabeth guessed her family was already in the rumour mill because of Mammi's loss. She didn't want to add a messy house to that or people would assume Elisabeth couldn't take care of her family.

She ran back into the kitchen and began slicing the sausage. Omama instructed Elisabeth to assemble a plate of food for Mammi, which Omama would take to her daughter herself. The rest of breakfast proceeded without a word. Omama, like Mammi, insisted that no one speak at the table. *At least one thing hasn't changed*, Elisabeth thought.

After clean-up, Elisabeth braided her hair fresh: one small braid on each side that was braided at the back with the rest of her hair. She pinned the long braid to the top of her head with a beautiful comb Maria had bought her from Arad, their county's city.

"Now, go outside," Omama said to Elisabeth. "Pull weeds—without getting dirty—or wipe down the flower boxes. Do something to look busy. Although we don't want you marrying any cousins, at the very least, they might bring a friend along. Do not come back inside until you smell like something nice. I'll hard-boil eggs for any boys who come by."

Omama reached to tap Elisabeth on the backside to make her hurry, but Elisabeth hurried out herself. She didn't need a physical reminder.

Once outside, Elisabeth felt stupid. She knew her neighbours would be watching, and besides, she was used to spending part of Easter Monday resting and enjoying time with visitors. However, Mammi still didn't want visitors inside the home, which Elisabeth understood. She went to the shed by the pig stalls and retrieved some clippers. The acacia tree at the front of their property needed trimming, and Elisabeth wouldn't get herself dirty doing it.

"What if no one comes?" she asked herself. "Then I'll be out here for hours, clipping a tree in my Sunday clothes." She closed the gate to the poultry yard behind her and entered the front yard. "And if only cousins come by, that would certainly be a waste of time." Maybe Omama's stay this week would be no different than her stay two months ago.

But if Elisabeth expected her siblings to listen to Omama, she would also have to. The sun shone, and the spring air was comfortably warm. It was a beautiful day to be spending time outside.

"I could also trim the plum and apricot trees at the back," she said to herself but realized Omama wanted her to spend her time at the front of the property. She sighed. "The acacia tree it is."

No sooner had she reached the tree, though, that she noticed someone walking up the street. Her cheeks turned red as she recognized Stefan.

But he's not a relative, she thought, *so why is he here? What if he's here for something serious?* Maybe Georg was having a fit again.

But as he came closer, the smile on his face told her nothing was wrong.

"Hello," he said.

"Hello." Elisabeth had butterflies in her stomach. Should she set the clippers down? Continue clipping the tree? Hold the clippers so she'd *look* busy?

Stefan leaned on the fence. "It's a lovely morning for a walk, so I thought I'd come by and see how your Easter was."

Now Elisabeth was confused. Stefan wasn't carrying any sort of bottle, though it would have looked a little silly for a grown man to spray her with a little perfume or rosewater. Besides, his parents and sister wouldn't have had to work today. Shouldn't he be spending the day with them?

"It was like a whirlwind," she replied with half a laugh. "We were at Peter-Bátschi's house."

At the mention of her uncle's name, Stefan's face darkened for a moment, but a gentle smile returned as quickly. "I'm certain it was. But you had a quiet evening afterwards?"

"Yes, we did."

Stefan and Elisabeth chatted for a little, talking more about Easter, Omama's visit, Mammi's condition, and the bribe Elisabeth had offered her siblings if they behaved all week.

Stefan pointed to the comb on her head. "That's very pretty. Is it a gift from Herr Schuhmacher?"

Elisabeth's cheeks burned. What did these feelings mean?

"From Frau Schuhmacher, then?" Stefan asked after she didn't reply.

Flustered, Elisabeth shook her head. "Um, no, no," she blurted out. "Maria gave it to me. She bought it in Arad."

Stefan smiled and Elisabeth's cheeks burned more.

Footsteps on the gravel street interrupted their conversation and Elisabeth's face cooled as she groaned inwardly. Toward their house came Andreas—one of Sophie-Néni and Peter-Bátschi's sons—and a friend of his, both holding little spray bottles in their hands. Couldn't they have come later?

"I get to spray her first!" Andreas shouted.

"Not if I beat you to her!" the other boy answered.

"Lissika, me first!" Andreas called to her. He did indeed reach her first. Just in time, Omama came out with a basket of hardboiled eggs.

After Andreas and then his friend lightly sprayed Elisabeth with their bottles of floral-scented perfume, Omama reached out the basket of eggs to them.

"Only one," she instructed.

"But can we get two if we spray Lissa-Néni?" Andreas asked.

Omama shook her head. "She's ill today." She then looked the friend up and down. "What's your name?"

"Kaiser Michael, Frau Braun," he answered.

"And how old are you?"

"Seventeen."

Omama nodded and Elisabeth knew what she was thinking.

"You may have a second egg," Omama said. Kaiser Michael helped himself to a second one, but when Andreas tried, Omama swatted his hand. "I'm certain your mother has boiled some at home." Kaiser Michael laughed at his friend.

She isn't offering Stefan one, Elisabeth thought.

Stefan extended his left hand to the two young men. "Schäfer Stefan."

"You're supposed to shake the right hand," Andreas said.

Kaiser Michael punched him in the shoulder. "You stupid cow, he doesn't have one."

"Oh, yeah," Andreas said with a giggle.

Stefan tucked his hand in his pocket. Elisabeth remembered his once saying how awkward it was to be the only man in the church without a complete body. Yes, once in a while a man might accidentally cut off the tip of a finger when working with sharp tools, but no one else had an arm that stopped before the elbow.

"Now, you boys, get," said Omama. "You've caused enough trouble. I trust we'll see you at the dance on Sunday?"

Andreas and his friend ran off down the street. "Yes, Omama!" Andreas called back. "Both of us!"

Omama waved after them.

That was it? Andreas was her grandson, too, and she said nothing about his rude behaviour!

"Nice to see you again, Herr Schäfer," Omama said with a disapproving look. "Come, Elisabeth, you've trimmed enough of the tree. Time to help me prepare lunch."

Elisabeth clenched her jaw at Omama's rudeness. She didn't even try to apologize for her grandson. *But at least I can.*

"Stefan, I'm sorry about my cousin—"

Stefan waved her concern away. "It's not the first time, I'm used to it." He smiled again, but his smile wasn't genuine.

"Come, Lissika, we have much to do this morning still."

Much to do? Omama had wanted Elisabeth to stay outside until some boy came by. Clearly, she was prepared to let her granddaughter stay outside for hours if necessary. Omama didn't want Elisabeth talking with Stefan.

Stefan doffed his cap. "Good day, Elisabeth."

"Will you be at Samuel's *salasch* tomorrow?"

At Omama's alarmed look, Stefan shrugged. "My parents may need me to tend to some chores around the house. The Haibachs expect them to head back to their *salasch* at the crack of dawn."

Grabbing her arm, Omama dragged Elisabeth back inside the house. Elisabeth's cheeks burned again, but for a much different reason. She pressed her lips together to prevent her words of anger from spilling out.

THE SECOND MORNING OF OMAMA'S STAY WAS WORSE, because Luki and Anna needed to get ready for school. Georg would arrive soon to take them, and Elisabeth would be on her way to the *salasch*. Seed had to be sown and the winter wheat soon harvested.

Elisabeth returned from the cellar out of breath with apricot jam. Rosina, already impatient with Omama's demands, threatened Elisabeth that she would tell Mammi about the lost baby if she couldn't have apricot jam today.

"Yesterday was apricot jam," she'd whispered to Elisabeth.

Knowing that Rosina didn't fully understand what losing a baby meant, and not wanting to explain the details to her, Elisabeth obeyed her six-year-old sister.

Anna finished setting the last plate on the table and everyone sat down.

"Now, whoever finishes first is the king!" Omama declared. The three children all dug in.

Elisabeth paused for a moment. Sandwiches had been packed for Anna and Luki, shoes polished, fingernails cleaned...

"Luki!" Elisabeth exclaimed.

"Shush!" Omama replied. "Or do you wish to wake up your mother?"

Elisabeth lowered her voice. "Luki, have you fed the animals this morning?"

Her brother's gaping mouth told her the answer. Luki stood up and Elisabeth told him to sit down again. "I'll take care of them. I can eat in the wagon."

"I can't be late," Anna said. "I don't care who feeds the animals, I can't be late. Herr Blum said that if I'm on time every day this week and know all my answers, he might sit me at the front of class again by Monday."

"We wouldn't be late if you would help me," Luki said, his arms crossed.

"I can't help you!" Anna replied, demonstrably pointing at her ankle.

"Must I repeat myself?" Omama raised her hand again.

"I'll be sure to finish before Georg arrives," Elisabeth said and shot her siblings warning looks.

Now Omama raised her voice. "Georg Schuhmacher? What is he coming here for?"

Silence fell over the Schuhmacher siblings. Elisabeth had hoped to not mention his name. Aside from Tata and Mammi, the Schuhmachers and Brauns did not care for one another, to put it mildly. Before the war changed Georg, he had called the Brauns "poor stock" and declared to everyone—including to Omama—that Mammi's first brother, Adam-Bátschi, had been killed in the war because he was not man enough to fend for himself. Not much later, Georg and Andreas-Bátschi were conscripted to fight, and Georg made another declaration: he would show everyone what a true man did and would protect Andreas-Bátschi.

But the fighting was more violent than anyone had imagined. Over the past couple of months, Elisabeth had learned—mostly through Stefan—the truth about fighting in the war. Georg and her uncle had developed a very strong friendship, to everyone's surprise, and Georg had written that he promised—the way a good man promised—to make sure Andreas-Bátschi came home.

What Omama, Mammi, Peter-Bátschi, and almost everyone else in their congregation would not accept, though, was that Georg had not been able to prevent Peter-Bátschi's death. Their ignorance pained Elisabeth the most. Georg relived the war in his mind every day, and often every night, but no one in Mammi's family ever showed him a word of kindness.

"Well?" Omama asked. "The devil follows that man wherever he goes. He has tricked your mother into allowing him to help you."

"No, he hasn't—"

"Shush. Go feed the animals. I'll see to it that the children are ready for school. Georg will *not* be taking the children in the wagon tomorrow. Luki can walk and Anna can stay home. Girls don't need to go to school, anyway."

Anna's jaw dropped opened and Omama waved for her to close it. "Your ankle is still sore. It's a good thing you didn't break it—I still can't walk straight on mine and it has been two years. But you can stay home and let it heal, so you can help with the household."

Elisabeth knew she would have to set Omama straight, but how? This was Mammi and Tata's family, not hers.

Mammi...Elisabeth had an idea.

"Mammi is proud that Anna sits at the front of the classroom, Omama. She works very hard in school and is the smartest one in the family. But because she missed several days after she hurt her ankle, Herr Blum put her in the second row."

Omama drew her lips into a straight line, just like Mammi, and then nodded. "I still think it's unwise, but if it makes my daughter feel better, then so be it."

Anna rejoiced.

"I'll hurry now," Elisabeth said. "I don't want to make you late."

"Oh, Lissika," Omama said. "You're staying here today."

"But the *salasch*—"

"If Georg insists on helping this family, he can take over your duties for today. Besides, if Stefan is there, then he has his extra help. I need you here. Now go feed the animals."

"But Stefan said—"

Omama raised her hand, ready to strike the granddaughter who had just been confirmed.

Anger rising inside her, Elisabeth went outside, not worrying if the door banged behind her. She grabbed an empty pail from the *hambar*, a roofed and fenced structure where corn for animal feed was stored. She pulled out a few cobs and scraped the kernels into the pail with a knife. The ducks began to quack, the geese to honk, and the chickens to cluck at the familiar sound. Elisabeth rushed to distribute the feed and returned the pail to its hook.

She doesn't want me seeing Stefan, I just know it! Elisabeth thought.

Behind the poultry yard stood the pigpen. Elisabeth pulled up one bucketful of water after another from their well, her anger driving her speed, and filled the pigs' troughs. But each bucket became heavier as her arms tired. As angry as she was at Omama, Elisabeth also wanted to finish Luki's morning chores and return to the kitchen to ensure the children had everything for school. Elisabeth would bring out the slop pail in a few hours, after she'd finished preparations for lunch.

Behind the cellar were the summer kitchen and work-shop, and then came the horse and cow stalls, with each building attached to the next in one row. (The outhouse came at the end.) Elisabeth ran to the horse and cow stalls and lifted hay into their stalls with a pitchfork.

She doesn't like him just because he has one arm. He's nice, honest, and he tells me things about the world and the war no one else does. Elisabeth had met Stefan only a few months ago, after his return from two years in Russian captivity in Siberia. As much as Elisabeth loved Semlak—it was where her heart lived—she also longed to hear about the bigger world. Stefan didn't refrain from telling her those stories, as most men would, and she liked that about him.

As she ran back to the house door, Georg pulled up in his wagon and Anna darted out on her crutches.

Elisabeth ran alongside her siblings, asking if they had packed everything. When they reached the wagon, Georg, one of the strongest men in the village, was already waiting behind it so he could lift Anna up.

Once Elisabeth caught up to everyone, he asked, "Is Frau Braun still here?"

Out of breath, Elisabeth could only nod.

Georg looked at the front windows, perhaps expecting to see Omama. He began to breathe faster and Elisabeth feared he would have another fit. She had never dealt with one by herself.

"Georg, we have to go!" Anna called out.

Georg nodded, walked around to the front, and swung himself up onto his horse. Unlike other German men, Georg did not ride on the wagon. Stefan and Samuel didn't know why, but after Georg had learned to ride a horse in the army, he always preferred it to sitting on the wagon.

"Are you not coming?" he asked Elisabeth.

"Omama wants me to stay here and help instead."

A rare but small, mischievous smile on his face, Georg said, "Stefan will be disappointed."

As Elisabeth's cheeks turned red at the mention of

Stefan's name, Georg's smile grew a little more. Elisabeth placed her hands on her cheeks—she was growing tired of how often they turned red. *I'd like to keep my feelings to myself, thank you,* she said to Jesus.

As Georg pulled away, Omama called her.

Great, now she's going to complain more about Georg, Elisabeth thought.

She didn't run, even though Omama was motioning for her to hurry. Once Elisabeth was standing in front of her grandmother, though, she regretted her decision. Elisabeth cried out in pain as Omama pulled on her ear.

"When I ask you to hurry, I expect you to listen. Your mother has woken up and has a fever. Go fetch the doctor immediately. After, you will go to my home and tell Peter-Bátschi that he is to pick you and your siblings up tomorrow. I will not have Georg setting foot on this property so long as I am here. Is that clear?" Omama let go of Elisabeth's ear, which now throbbed. "Is that clear?"

Elisabeth nodded and ran off again, her stomach rumbling and her head aching. She still hadn't eaten breakfast and now Mammi needed her help.

Was this what it meant to keep the family together?

CHAPTER NINE

In the hour since she had returned home from school, Juliana had accomplished nothing.

"Juliana?" Mom knocked on the door and entered. "What are you studying?"

Juliana had a lie ready: "English. We've got a test in a few days. About perspective."

Mom nodded, seeming to consider her answer. "It's really good how early they're teaching that now, but your studying will be more effective if you write things out."

Again, Juliana lied. "Oh, no, I didn't know that." She followed with something truthful. "You know me: I like to rehearse things out loud." Then another lie. "But I'm just quiet today." One true statement out of three was okay for lying to parents, right?

"Well, keep going. Looks like you're doing better." Mom smiled and closed the door behind her.

Juliana's stomach tightened into a knot. Yes, she'd lied to her parents before and didn't even worry about guilt. But she'd lied about things like sneaking chocolate from the Halloween stash to wake up her brain and study another half hour. Or saying she had sorted the recycling when she had dumped it in the trash can and tied up the bag to have more time to study. Juliana's moral code allowed her to lie in order to study, but not to lie that she *was* studying.

Two weeks ago, when she couldn't talk to her family about what troubled her, she'd spoken to Rachel. *She deserves a break from being my best friend for a little,* Juliana thought. *Besides, she'll tell me to talk to my parents or aunt, anyway.* She didn't want to talk to Uncle Peter either, even if he'd been in town.

Dad would tell Mom for sure. Juliana didn't want to worry Sophie, especially after Opa had hallucinated in front of them once, frightening Sophie enough. Jasmine's comments from the other night still hurt, and Juliana needed to spend more time with her new friends at school before talking to them about something like this.

"What about Elisabeth?" Juliana asked herself. "Her stories have helped me a lot." She pulled out her great-grandmother's sketchbook and a notebook she'd used for notes in past months. She opened the notebook to the last page she'd written on and pulled out an old photo and the translation of an unfinished letter of Elisabeth's.

In the photo lay a woman in a simple coffin, a wooden grave marker beside her, and several people standing behind her, their hands folded in prayer. When Opa had shown it to Juliana the first time, she almost choked on her food: she wasn't used to seeing *real* photos of dead people. Her notes in her notebook said, "Susanna Schubkegel, 1903-1934."

"Opa said that Elisabeth wasn't in the photo probably because she took it," Juliana said out loud. "He told me she liked new things. So, Elisabeth most likely still lived in Semlak at that time." She recorded her note.

This was the only photograph Juliana had seen of Opa's family. All the women wore headscarves and the men, hats. *Almost like the Mennonites around here*, she thought. Her notes listed the names of the family members standing behind Susanna, all members of Opa's great-uncle's family, including Georg and his wife, Eva. Susanna was Georg's sister.

Georg must have been sad when she died, Juliana thought. *She was only thirty-one years old.* Juliana didn't have any siblings, but she'd be sad if anyone in her family died at that age. *I wonder what she died from?*

Juliana turned to the translation of Elisabeth's unfinished letter. Juliana and Sophie had found the original letter in the encyclopedia Sophie had dropped. Juliana had learned that day that Uncle Peter spoke and read German. They had returned the original letter to its resting place, but Uncle Peter had taken photos and later emailed the girls his translation.

Juliana began reading.

March 12, 1920

   Dear Tata,

   Thank you for your postcard. It was a wonderful surprise! We were all very happy to hear from you.

   I wish I could write you and say that I am doing well, but I am not. I have been studying hard for my confirmation

Juliana chuckled and put the letter down. "Even Elisabeth is telling me to study." She returned the artefacts to the notebook. "Schuhmacher History," she said to herself. "To be continued."

She ran her hand over the hard leather cover of Elisabeth's journal. *I'm not doing well either,* she thought. *I quit the dance club at school, I'm lying to Mom, and my marks are horrific. I don't even know who I am anymore.*

The sense of disappointment in herself that had appeared after quitting the dance club earlier grew. She couldn't even look herself in the mirror.

Dad had called her two days ago to ask how she was doing. Maybe if she asked politely, he wouldn't tell Mom right away. She stared at her phone, her finger ready to touch his number. *He'll understand, won't he?* she thought. What other option did she have? Her mind continued to fixate on the man from the old-age home.

She dialled.

"Hey, sweetie. How are things?" Dad's voice was cheery but tinny because the call was on speaker. The noise of the engine vibrating through the truck's cab served as a backdrop to their call. Had it always been that loud?

"Pretty good," she answered, but as soon as the words slipped out, Juliana knew she didn't sound convincing.

"No, you're not," Dad replied. His horn blasted in the background. "Sorry. Another hyper-miler just cut in to tailgate the truck in front of me. Give me a sec." Juliana listened as Dad radioed his company's dispatch to try to contact the driver of the other truck and notify him of a car in his blindspot. "Stupid idiot. I'm back. Sorry, Jules, but I can tell in your voice something's up. Plus, *you're* calling *me*. I know we're almost a thousand kilometres apart, but you can still talk to me."

Juliana took a deep breath and said, "I quit the dance club today."

"Really?" Dad sounded surprised. "But you were so excited about it."

"I know. But you were right, it was too much."

"That's not the real reason. Try again."

Mom called down the hallway. "Juliana! No phone calls! You should be studying!"

Juliana covered the microphone but didn't think hit mute as she replied through her door. "I'm talking to Meghan about English!" Juliana held her breath: would Mom remember that Meghan didn't take English class with her?

"Ten minutes!" came the reply.

"Okay!" Juliana said.

Dad's voice was stern. "Jules, what's going on? If I recall, Meghan is *not* in your English class. You'd better explain yourself. Now. I don't want to lie to my wife."

The conversation was not going as planned, if thinking about it for five seconds before dialling counted as planning.

Juliana took another deep breath, this time to push away the tears threatening to burst through. "I saw...the old-age home..." Telling Dad no longer scared her, but where should she start?

"Was it hard to see some of the people there?" Dad asked, his voice now gentle.

"Yeah. I mean, I was certain I could smell pee, and this one guy who seemed...paralyzed. I don't know. He didn't move. But his head was tilted to one side, his mouth was open, and he had a bib..." She swallowed a sob.

"It sounds like it was a bit of a surprise for you. You've never been in a long-term care facility before, have you?"

Juliana grabbed a tissue, dried her eyes, and dabbed at her nose. "But is that how Opa...?" She sniffled.

Dad let out a big sigh. "No one really knows, sweetie. Aging isn't always pretty."

"That's what Jasmine said."

"So you've talked to her already? What else did she tell you?"

"That there was nothing I could do about it and that there are worse things and that I should get out of my bubble."

Did Juliana really live in a bubble? Was she overreacting again? If so, why couldn't she stop?

"Juliana!" Mom shouted. "Seven minutes!"

Mom was timing her?

"Okay!" Juliana shouted back. She then lay on her bed and covered her head with a pillow so Mom wouldn't hear her talking to Dad.

"Mom again?" Dad asked.

"Yeah. But I can't tell her this kind of thing. I mean, it's her dad."

"I see that now."

"Did your parents live in an old-age home?"

Another pause, and Juliana wondered if she shouldn't have asked. Dad rarely talked about his family. His answer confirmed her suspicion. "It's called a long-term care facility or a nursing home. I'm not saying that to be picky, but it'll hopefully help you see that they're places people go to get care, not to age. But no, my parents didn't. They both died in their forties."

"What? How? I mean, you've never told me."

"That's a conversation for another time. But I understand now why you're so upset."

Juliana wanted to talk to Dad about everything, but she couldn't bring herself to explain the rest. If Dad could help erase the image of the man in the nursing home from her mind, then everything else would be fine: she could stop worrying, start studying, catch up, and not have to tell Mom about any of this.

"Listen," Dad said. "I'm home late tomorrow afternoon. When do you have dance again?"

"Not until next week. Easter weekend, remember?"

"Sorry—I forgot. Hours on the road make you lose track of time. I'll be home by five or so tomorrow. Let's talk then, okay?"

Juliana sighed. "Sure." Same thing each time, Dad pushing off conversations until later because of work. To some extent, Juliana understood—any time she read about a tractor-trailer accident on social media, she worried it might be Dad. She didn't want him driving distracted, but she still wanted to talk to him.

"This is something easier to talk about in person," Dad said. The tone in his voice suggested he'd heard her disappointment. "I need to see you, and I don't want to worry about choppy video and stuff. I won't tell your mom about tonight—I understand why you don't want to talk to her.

We will need to tell her how you've been feeling, but we'll wait until you're ready."

"Okay. Thank you."

"I love you."

"Yeah. Sure."

"We'll work through this. I know this is tough, but it's easier to talk in person. We will talk about it tomorrow, Jules, I promise."

"Okay."

Dad hung up.

She imagined the cracks in the egg of Elisabeth's drawing spreading. This was why Juliana had such a hard time with Dad: He was never around when she needed him.

Juliana didn't take the pillow off her head. She didn't want Mom to hear her crying.

CHAPTER TEN

By Wednesday morning, the Schuhmachers had gotten used to Omama's routine, and everyone was ready for the day on time. Mammi was sitting at the table in the front room, her fever gone, embroidering the satin upper of a woman's dress shoe with her intricate floral patterns. Luki sat opposite Mammi, playing with Tata's deck of cards, his chores already done. Rosina was putting away dishes in the kitchen with Omama. Would today be a calm day? And would Elisabeth be allowed to tend the family farmland? Omama had said nothing all morning, so Elisabeth assumed the answer was yes and packed her things.

"That looks lovely," Elisabeth said of Mammi's handiwork.

"The workshop is too dark," Mammi said. "Stefan built

a fine stove, but one door and some lanterns do not let in as much light as two windows. I can embroider better here."

Tata had built his workshop into the summer kitchen—between the cellar and horse and cow stalls—and did not include a window. An open door provided the only source of daylight. About a month ago, Stefan had built Mammi a small heating stove in the workshop so the door could stay open more. He wanted to show other villagers that he could work despite having only one arm. So far as Elisabeth knew, though, nobody would pay him because he worked slower than a man with two arms. Although Stefan helped on Samuel's *salasch*, he refused to accept payment from friends. His parents and sister worked as day labourers on the Haibach farm this year. Elisabeth would make sure to organize an evening for *majen* soon—when Mammi was well—and she would invite Stefan's sister.

"I'm glad to hear you like his work, Mammi," Elisabeth said. "Maybe you know of anyone who might hire him...?"

Still staring at her work, Mammi shook her head. "No one will pay for a man who's missing an arm, Lissika, you know that. It's easier finding work as a woman."

"Then he can be paid less. He just wants to support his family."

"His family? Or his future family?"

"I suppose both."

Mammi shook her head as she turned the piece of satin around to sew in another spot. "Lord have pity on that man.

Without work, he cannot find a wife, and no wealthy family will want to give him their money."

"That doesn't seem fair at all," Elisabeth said. "After fighting and then being imprisoned in Siberia, he can't work or find a wife? How is that just?"

Before Mammi answered, Anna hobbled in on her crutches, a scowl on her face.

"I'm not going to get back to the front of the classroom," she said, her gaze fixed on the two front windows. "Where is he?" She paced along the floor between the table in the centre of the room and the settee and beds against the back wall. Elisabeth inwardly lamented about all the divots she would have to smooth out of the dirt-and-chaff floor when she and her sisters (and Omama?) cleaned the house on Saturday.

"Anna, stop that pacing," Mammi complained. "You're giving me a headache."

"But Peter-Bátschi's late!"

"Anna!" Elisabeth scolded. "You don't talk like that about family!"

Anna glowered back at her older sister.

Elisabeth walked past Omama and Rosina in the kitchen, and to the back room, where the clock stood on a chest of drawers. Anna was right: Peter-Bátschi was at least fifteen minutes late. Elisabeth reported the time and returned to the front room, wondering if Anna would leave the front room if Elisabeth asked her. She didn't want to risk her sister disobeying her in front of Omama, but at the same time, Anna was annoying Mammi, who was still not well.

"There he is!" Anna pointed out the window and Elisabeth offered a private prayer of thanks to Jesus.

Peter-Bátschi sauntered through the gates, past the house, and to the stalls, not even saying hello first.

Anna raced into the kitchen, but Elisabeth told her to wait for their uncle to hitch up the horse.

"But I'm going to be late!"

"If you rush outside, you'll still have to wait for him. *Be patient.*" She whispered in Anna's ear, "Remember, cookies. With icing decorations." Anna closed her mouth.

Luki took his time coming to the door. He didn't particularly like school. *He's probably happy to be late*, Elisabeth thought.

"Modr, say what you will about Georg, but at least he has the decency to come on time," Mammi said to Omama.

Elisabeth wasn't sure she'd heard her mother right: Had Mammi said something nice about Georg?

Omama flapped her hand at her daughter. "I will not hear that horrible man's name so long as I'm in this house," she said. "He's an embarrassment to your husband's family."

"Modr, what should embarrass you is that Georg has helped us much more than Peter ever has."

Elisabeth hadn't misheard.

Omama adjusted the knot under her headscarf. "It's because of the war." With that she returned to the kitchen and began peeling potatoes, ending the conversation.

Elisabeth needed a moment to remember what she still needed to do. That Mammi had said something nice about her nephew truly surprised Elisabeth.

"Luki, Anna, come. Let's let Mammi rest. Peter-Bátschi should be almost ready."

"When will you get better?" Rosina asked.

"Soon," Mammi said.

Elisabeth thought so, too. The colour in her cheeks had returned that morning, making Mammi look much better than yesterday and certainly better than on Saturday, when her pain left her unable to even walk. The sooner Mammi got better, the sooner Omama would go home and Elisabeth's life would return to normal. Elisabeth knew she was supposed to love Omama, but did that mean she had to love having her in the house? She asked Jesus, not expecting any answer, though. He never gave her one.

"Now, Lissika," Omama said. "You will return from the *salasch* this afternoon, with your brother and sister. Peter-Bátschi will collect you first and then the children at school. You will help me around the house and this evening visit my home: Little Sophie has invited friends over and a friend of Peter and Sophie's will be showing you some crocheting. Take your best crochet work along. I'm surprised Lissa has not sent you out yet this year. How does she expect you to impress women who might find a good match for you?"

When could Elisabeth have found the time to go out? With her fervent studying for her confirmation and all the chores she had to do without Mammi's help, she hadn't had a moment to spare to visit with friends and family during the week. Granted, as much as Elisabeth enjoyed spending time with friends, she did not miss the weekly gossip at these gatherings. *On the other hand*, she thought, *if it's one evening I don't have to spend here, I should be thankful.* But was an evening at Peter-Bátschi and Sophie-Néni's house any better than at her own right now?

"Little Sophie has taken care to invite Maria," Omama added.

That pleased Elisabeth. "Thank you."

Elisabeth helped her siblings get dressed. Yes, she had to tolerate the ride out to the *salasch* with her uncle, but at least she would see Stefan, Georg, Samuel, and Deaf-Lissi shortly. Even just a few hours of their company would make her happy.

Georg. Mammi had actually said something nice about him. Elisabeth thanked Jesus for the small miracle as she rushed to get her shawls and headscarf and followed her siblings out the door.

Elisabeth fought to contain her thoughts as she trudged down the dirt road that led to the Schuhmacher *salasch*. Jesus would be unhappy with those thoughts, but the words kept pushing against her will.

All farmland in Semlak lay outside the village, as it did for all villages of the former Austrian-Hungarian Empire, so far as Elisabeth knew. The Schuhmacher *salasch* began about four kilometres north of Semlak with others as far as ten kilometres outside the village. Those who lived on their *salasch* only travelled to town for market on Tuesdays simply to save time and energy. Therefore, Pastor Fröhlich held a special midweek service for them.

Elisabeth had never heard of anyone spending only a few hours on a *salasch*. Whenever her family traveled to their farmland, they spent the entire day tending to the seven acres Tata had inherited from his father. A few hours' work wasn't much longer than the entire time she would spend traveling there and back.

Or shorter when your uncle doesn't come out of the tavern and you have to walk half the way, she thought.

The words Elisabeth had been trying to bury surfaced.

I hate him. She glanced behind her to see if her uncle was coming—something she had done the whole way. No sign of him.

"Elisabeth!" someone called from up ahead. Her mood lifted when she saw Stefan smiling and waving his cap at her. She picked up her pace.

Stefan stood in the poultry yard of the *salasch*, a leather sack hanging from his neck. He threw a handful of corn at the birds and let himself out to greet Elisabeth at the road.

"I'm so sorry!" she called out.

"We were expecting you over an hour ago," he said. "Is everything all right?"

Elisabeth leaned on the fence. Having to walk two kilometres from the tavern to the *salasch* had drained her of some of the energy she'd hoped to save for working in the fields.

"Where's Peter?" Stefan asked.

Elisabeth fought back a growl as she answered. "At the tavern."

Stefan's jaw dropped. "What?"

"He stopped at the tavern on our way here and said he wasn't going to be long. I don't know how long I waited, but it was long enough."

Stefan shook his head. "The drinking. The war did that to him, but he won't stop."

"He'd better learn how because he's not helping my family at all." Elisabeth removed her headscarf and brushed back some of the hair that had fallen out of her braids. She tied her headscarf back on. "It's our horse and wagon out there," she said. "If I knew how to drive a wagon, I could've come out here myself."

Stefan returned to the poultry yard and Elisabeth followed him. When they entered the chicken area, Elisabeth grabbed a handful of corn from the leather sack around his neck and threw it on the ground. The chickens clucked as they walked around, pecking at the fallen grain.

"Could you or Georg or Samuel show me how to drive a wagon?" Elisabeth asked. "We'll still need your help picking Luki and Anna up on days when I'm here, but at least they'd arrive at school on time. Omama still...you know." She reached for another handful of corn and threw it at the chickens.

"There was truly nothing Georg could've done," Stefan said. "It was war. Had he disobeyed their commanding officer, he might have been shot." He threw out another handful himself and moved on to the duck compound. Elisabeth followed.

"What's done is done, I guess, on all fronts." She reached for another handful of corn kernels. "But why are you out here? Isn't Deaf-Lissi feeling well?" Women fed the fowl. Stefan had only one arm, but he didn't need to do women's work.

Elisabeth threw the kernels in an arc on the ground, and some ducks waddled to the nearest grains while others came to Elisabeth's feet, waiting for more.

He shrugged. "I wanted to be helpful."

They left the ducks and headed over to the geese, who were honking loudly at the coming food.

"Doesn't Georg need your help?" Elisabeth said over the noise. "I would have found you."

Stefan stopped, glanced at Elisabeth, scratched his neck, and stared at his boots. "Well, to be honest, I wanted to wait for you."

Her face had never heated up so fast. Did he mean that? She liked Stefan, too, despite what Mammi had said. *These feelings happen every time I see him*, she thought. *That's what they mean.*

"Ow!" she cried out. A goose had nipped at her ankle. She and Stefan laughed.

The *clip-clip* of the horse's hooves distracted Elisabeth from the task at hand.

"Keep your hands relaxed, because the horse can feel if you pull and will begin to turn," Georg said. To show Elisabeth how to drive a wagon, he sat next to her on the driver's bench instead of on the horse.

Her uncle had never come, so she and Georg had driven to the school to pick up her siblings. Her head ached from the anger she felt about Peter-Bátschi's broken promises. She only hoped Luki hadn't left Anna behind and walked home without her.

As they came up to a crossroads, Georg helped her pull on the reins to turn right, and the horse followed.

"She also knows the way," he explained of the horse. "I'm sure yours must, too."

They passed flat farmland as far as the eye could see as the horse continued on its way.

"We really only need one horse," Elisabeth said. "And maybe one cow and two pigs. Without Tata here, we don't need so many animals."

"Have you told Lissa-Néni?"

Elisabeth shook her head. "Mammi has been healing from her loss." Tears formed in her eyes and rolled down her cheeks. She tried wiping her cheeks on her shoulders since her hands held the reins, but once Georg noticed, he passed her a handkerchief from his pocket and lifted the reins out of her hands.

"Why am I the only one crying about the baby?" she asked as she dried her eyes.

"You haven't been hardened by life but you're also old enough to understand."

"I hate it."

"It could be worse."

Georg's words echoed in her mind like a branch scraping at a window. At first Elisabeth wanted to demand what could be worse than losing a baby. She came to her senses, though, before she said something rude, when she recalled the few war experiences Stefan had told her about: body parts flying everywhere when a bomb landed, and friends begging for help even though their comrades knew they were going to die. At one battle, Georg and Andreas-Bátschi had been separated by their commanding officer.

After night had fallen and Georg couldn't find his best friend among those who'd returned, he searched the field infirmary. Stefan wouldn't tell Elisabeth much more than to say that Andreas-Bátschi had been unconscious and had died not much later.

To lose a wife and their first child on top of all of that, Elisabeth thought. *He's probably frightened he'll lose Eva and their unborn child, too.* Things could indeed be worse.

She returned his handkerchief and he handed her back the reins. They neared the next major crossroads, where the tavern was, and Elisabeth looked for her horse and wagon.

Nothing.

"I hope he at least took everything home again," she said. *And that he has already left.* Elisabeth was certain no amount of strength from Jesus would help her contain her anger if she saw her uncle again.

CHAPTER ELEVEN

Juliana had managed to calm herself by supper.

"How's your studying coming along?" Mom asked as she opened the microwave and brought a bowl of steaming broccoli to the table.

"Um, good. Test tomorrow. I think I'm ready."

Mom smiled. "You'll get those marks up again. You just need to focus a bit more. I suppose dance and studying aren't that different from one another, are they?"

Juliana nodded her head in agreement. Mom speared the chicken breasts in the frying pan and dropped them on to a plate.

"It smells wonderful, wonderful. *So sagt der Lawrence Welk*," Opa said and Mom laughed.

At Juliana's confused expression, Mom explained:

"Lawrence Welk had a TV show a really long time ago. I can't remember when it ended. Polka music, band music, easy listening, that kind of thing. But he was German-American so he was popular here, too. And he always said, 'wonderful, wonderful.'"

All three began to serve themselves broccoli, chicken, and quinoa.

"And he had tap dancing, too," Opa added. "I think that's actually where Katy first saw it."

"Really?" Mom asked. "I don't remember anymore."

Opa nodded confidently and Mom looked pleased at having learned something about her childhood she'd forgotten.

"Where's the *ding*?" Opa asked. Just like Opa never said "Juliana" with a *j* sound, he never said the English word for "remote." He always said "the *ding*." But if Juliana said "remote" to him, he understood. "Ever since you bought me this fancy TV for my birthday, I can't find the *ding*. It's too skinny."

Mom reached to the slick flat-screen TV behind her and passed the remote to Opa. "But do we have to watch now?" she asked. "It's nice to just eat together, and I wouldn't mind knowing what else I've forgotten about my childhood."

But Opa turned on the television set. "Karl's on the news. They're talking about cancer and the rubber factories again."

Great, Juliana thought. *The last thing I need to hear about is cancer.* Judging by the opening teasers, though, it looked like the segment was going to be on first. *At least we can turn this off afterwards.*

The picture changed to that of a man.

"That's Karl!" Opa said, his face beaming with pride. Juliana smiled a little—Opa was cute when he got this excited.

A correspondent's voice introduced the segment. "'Enough is enough,' says this man, one of thousands still living who've been affected by cancer allegedly caused by working in a local rubber factory."

"I've already had cancer once," Karl said to the reporter.

"And you're in remission now?"

"*Ja*, but I'm scared every day that it will come back."

The correspondant faced the camera. "Karl Wagner believes his cancer was caused by spending almost twenty years working at a local rubber factory. And he's not alone. This man..."

Juliana's mind tuned out the rest and began to obsess over one thought: Opa had worked with Karl in the same factory. Would Opa get cancer, too? She swallowed her food—she didn't want Mom and Opa knowing what worried her—but her stomach began to churn.

A rustle of paper interrupted her never-ending fear as Opa whipped open today's newspaper.

"And look at this, Yulika!" he said, tapping on a two-page spread of headshots. "All of these people have died from cancer, too, in these factories and they're not getting a single penny. I know..." He began rhyming off names, and Juliana tried to figure out how to nonchalantly excuse herself from the table.

Mom interrupted Opa's speech. "Tata, you're in perfect health except for your brain. You had tests for cancer a few weeks ago, and the doctor said everything was fine."

Juliana breathed out. *Everything was fine.*

"But that doesn't mean I'll never get it," he insisted. "I'm one year closer to dying now. Maybe I'll die from cancer. You young people don't worry about these things."

"I have to get ready for dance," Juliana said and rushed to her room. Neither Opa nor Mom called after her.

Juliana lay on her side on her bed, her knees pulled up. What if Opa did get cancer? Juliana remembered that Opa had mentioned this worry about cancer a few times over the past few months. Juliana hadn't thought much of it until now.

"Until I saw that man at the home," she realized, "I honestly thought Opa would just lose his memory a little bit here, a little bit there, probably get extra angry some-times...I didn't think he'd..." The rest of her sentence stayed stuck in her throat, because she felt that saying those worries out loud would make them real. She tried to bury them in a corner of her mind where she could lock them up and be happy again, like she had been when Mom and Opa were joking after his birthday party at the club on the weekend.

But her mind resisted and cracks spread as the words worked their way back to her awareness. Her stomach contracted, but she kept its contents in place. "I still can't believe I told Rachel at my goodbye party that Mom and her family should put Opa in a home."

Juliana had never felt so angry with herself. She'd rather freeze on stage in the middle of a dance at a national competition than remember the mean words she had said about her grandfather.

"And then I told Mom what I'd said to Rachel. I can't take that back."

Her nausea became stronger.

"Juliana?" Mom knocked on the door and opened up. "Are you ready...? Jules? What's wrong?"

Juliana jumped off her bed, raced past Mom, and slammed the door to the bathroom behind her.

CHAPTER TWELVE

Georg sat atop his horse while Elisabeth sat in the wagon with her siblings. She'd asked him to drive once they reached the school because she didn't know if Mammi would approve of her learning to drive a wagon, and she didn't want to risk Anna and Luki spilling the beans. That they hadn't mentioned anything yet about babies was already a stroke of kindness from God.

As they pulled up in front of their gate, the house door burst open, and Peter-Bátschi came storming out. His face was red and his short hair was tousled. He fumbled with the latch on each gate.

"Do you know how long I waited for you?" he yelled at Elisabeth. "I searched everywhere for you! I was worried I'd lost you!"

Elisabeth's siblings wrapped their arms around each other fearfully. *The same way they used to react to Georg*, she thought.

"I waited two hours!" Peter-Bátschi yelled.

Omama hobbled out of the house and called for her son, but he ignored her.

"I asked everyone in the tavern if they'd seen you, and they all laughed at me!"

What right did her uncle have to yell at her like that when he hadn't even fulfilled his duties? "Where did you think I'd gone?" She climbed over the side of the wagon and instructed her siblings to go inside immediately, but they stayed bolted to each other.

"How was I supposed to know?" Peter-Bátschi shouted back. "Maybe with some boy!"

Elisabeth glowered at her uncle. "How dare you say such a thing about me!"

Omama, too, shouted at her son for accusing Elisabeth of such dishonourable behaviour.

"So you forgot?" Elisabeth asked him. "You were to take me to my family's land. I had no time to wait for you! I had *duties* to tend to!"

She turned around and told her siblings again to get out, but they didn't move, their knees now pulled up tightly against their chests.

Georg jumped down from the horse and took hold of

the reins to steady it, but Peter-Bátschi lunged toward him and shoved him.

"You're the one teaching her to shout like this!"

Georg grunted as his back slammed into the side of the wagon. The horse neighed and stumbled backwards.

"Peter, you fool!" Omama shouted as she shuffled toward the street. "The children haven't gotten out yet!"

Ignoring his mother, Peter-Bátschi swung for Georg's face, but Georg ducked.

"You'll cause the horse to panic," Georg said.

"Do you think I care about your horse?" He swung at Georg again, getting him in the arm. "Oh, wait, you're a crazy man. How would you know the answer to that?" Peter-Bátschi swung at Georg a third time, hitting him in the arm again.

How could he aim so well while he was so drunk? Peter-Bátschi had fought Stefan once, and her uncle had missed every time. But after another swing, Elisabeth found her answer: Georg was deliberately placing himself between the horse and Peter-Bátschi to try to keep the horse calm.

Finally reaching the men, Omama took over the reins. "Peter, stop this!" She continued yelling at her son.

Elisabeth took advantage of the distraction. "Luki, you out first. Quick. Omama has the horse. Then we'll help Anna." Luki stood up, but the wagon lurched and he fell back down. Out of the corner of her eye, Elisabeth saw

Georg move along the fence, away from the horse and wagon, one hand pressing on his back.

"Because of you, my friends called me a stupid cow!" Elisabeth's uncle shouted at her cousin.

Luki jumped out of the wagon and Anna passed him both her crutches.

"You can do it," Elisabeth said, holding her hand out to her sister. Anna raised herself onto her knees and the wagon rocked again, sending her back onto her bottom with a cry.

The stern expression on Omama's face told Elisabeth she was doing her best to hold the horse steady. She stroked its mane and spoke calmly to it.

Elisabeth nodded to Anna and reached her hand out again. Luki stood next to the wagon, too, his feet spread to steady himself. Anna was lifting her sprained ankle over the edge of the wagon when the wagon rocked again. She fell into Elisabeth's arms, knocking them both to the ground. Omama's face turned red but she stayed silent, continuing to try to control the horse.

Luki bent down, his face serious like the man he wanted to be. "Anna, are you all right?" He held out one hand and in his other hand offered her a crutch.

Peter-Bátschi continued yelling at Georg.

Luki helped his sister off Elisabeth, who scrambled to her feet. Being on the ground behind the wagon was dangerous: they needed to get out of the way fast.

"Get away now!" she called to Luki, grabbing Anna under her arms and dragging her a few metres away just before the wagon rolled back to the spot where they had fallen.

"Why is Peter-Bátschi shouting?" Anna asked. "*He* forgot *us*."

Luki reached for her crutches. "He's angry, like Georg gets angry," he said, "but he's angry at real people."

"Get inside," Elisabeth told her siblings. She didn't want to ignore their questions, but they could wait. Each time they turned around to watch the fight, she waved them in again. "Remember what I promised you this weekend!" she shouted after them, but they still walked slower than snails.

Elisabeth spied her neighbour pretending to prune her flowers but in truth staring at the fight, soaking in every detail so she could share it with her friends in an hour or two. What business was this of hers? But Elisabeth forced herself to return her attention to the two men.

Peter-Bátschi kept swinging at Georg, who continued moving toward the house, drawing his opponent away from the horse. "You weren't there," Georg said, his voice even. "Someone had to help them. Frau Braun wanted Elisabeth home—"

"Just like you weren't there for my brother," Peter-Bátschi seethed and tripped over his own feet as he threw another punch at Georg.

Elisabeth took the reins from Omama, led Georg's horse farther away from the fight, and tied the reins to the fence.

"Peter, that's enough!" Omama said.

She pushed the two younger children through the gates to the poultry yard and straight toward the house, where Rosina was peeking out of the house door, clutching a doll to her chest.

"He couldn't help Andreas-Bátschi!" Elisabeth shouted. "You'd understand that if you'd listen to him!"

Elisabeth's attempt at defending Georg distracted her cousin, and Peter-Bátschi used the moment to ram him into the second fence. Georg grunted as his back slammed into a post.

"You coward. You won't even fight me. You're scared as a mouse," Peter-Bátschi said as he rocked back and forth, unable to steady his balance. "You even need a girl to fight for you."

"Peter!" Mammi marched from the back of the house, one hand around her belly. Had she been in the workshop today? "What is so important that you have to tell our business to all the neighbours?"

"Georg stopped his work to help us," Elisabeth explained to her mother.

"I'm well aware of that," Mammi said. "You can't fulfill your duties for even one day," she said to her brother. "Just go home. Leave us all in peace."

Elisabeth had never heard such an ugly laugh from her uncle. "Leave *you* in peace?" He pointed to Georg. "With this crazy man? How about he goes and leaves us in peace!"

"No one is on your side," Mammi said. "Just go."

"It's because you've all got a bird in your head," he said, tapping his skull.

"No, we don't!" Elisabeth insisted.

From behind her, Georg repeated in a low voice, "He's drunk, Lissika. You can't reason with him." Louder and to Peter-Bátschi, he said, "Let me walk you home, Peter. You need to sleep."

Peter-Bátschi laughed the same evil laugh, sending chills down Elisabeth's spine.

"Lissa," Peter-Bátschi said to his sister. "This mouse wants to walk me home. I'll squash it under my boot before that happens."

Mammi's response surprised Elisabeth. "With the way you've been acting, I think it's a wise idea for Georg to take you home. You're so drunk, you couldn't tell the difference between a pig and a horse."

"He might kill me, Lissa. He fakes his fits so he can show us all who he's going to kill next. Do you want another dead brother?"

Omama hobbled out of the house and approached them, holding Peter-Bátschi's hat.

Mammi lost her patience and slapped her brother's cheek. Startled, Peter-Bátschi stared at his sister.

"We can't even ask you to take the children to school on time," she said. "You're useless to your family so long as you drink like a fish in a flood."

Elisabeth's uncle straightened his jacket. "Now you're offending me," he said. "I can take a lot of insults, but not a slap from one of my sisters." He glared at her.

"You should be offended," Mammi said, not moving a centimetre. "If I'm telling you that Georg has to take care of you, you're the one with the problem. Fix it!"

"There's nothing wrong with me," Peter-Bátschi insisted.

"Peter, you're dumber than a donkey," Omama said. "You can't even walk straight. Now all the neighbours are staring at us, and for once, Georg looks like the normal man. Go home, apologize to your wife, and go to sleep." She handed him his hat. "Go before I slap you, too. I'm still your mother."

Peter-Bátschi yanked his hat out of Omama's hand. After several attempts to place it on his head, he grumbled something no one understood, held the hat in his hand, and began stumbling home.

Georg rubbed where his back had hit the wagon and fence. "I'll return for the horse and wagon." He followed Elisabeth's drunken uncle, staying back far enough that Peter-Bátschi didn't seem to notice him.

As the men's footsteps disappeared down the street, Elisabeth, Mammi, and Omama all stared at the ground.

For three women with tempers, silence was rare. Elisabeth asked Jesus for forgiveness, but how else should she have behaved? Even Mammi and Omama had shouted.

Oh no, Elisabeth thought. *I'm supposed to go to Omama's house this evening for* majen. What she really needed was a quiet night alone with her sketchbook and perhaps one of Martin Luther's sermons. Elisabeth didn't want to see her uncle again unless it was for him to apologize. But not today, no matter what he might say to her.

"Omama," she said, her voice low. "Please forgive me for asking, but I—"

Omama didn't let her finish. "I ask very little of my children," she said, sadness in her voice. "Follow the Word of the Lord and fulfill your duties to your family and our church." Elisabeth had never seen such a look of disgust on Omama's face as she glanced in the direction of her son. Even when she was angry with Elisabeth or her siblings, that expression had never appeared. "That Georg has to walk my son home...I can't show my face at church on Sunday."

"Georg has been helpful to us," Elisabeth said, her voice steady but quiet.

Mammi released her arm from around her belly and took a deep breath. "Modr, Lissika is telling the truth. It hurts to say it, but she is."

Omama shook her head at her daughter. "Lissa, I can

see the pain on your face every time that horrible man comes near you. The doctor said you still need your rest."

Mammi replied, "Georg may not have known his duty before or during the war, but he knows it now. We can't ignore that."

More silence followed, and Elisabeth felt out of place. Any talk about the two brothers Mammi had lost in that great war seemed like it belonged to only Mammi and Omama. The war had left holes in all families in Semlak, maybe not always in a home, but definitely in everyone's hearts and memories. Elisabeth wondered if she should find an excuse to return to the house, perhaps by saying she needed to check on her siblings. But one look toward the house erased that idea: their faces were pressed against the windows in the front room.

Mammi broke the silence. "I have just lost a baby, and it was probably the last baby Lukas and I will ever have. The problems Peter caused today are the last things I need. Let Georg take the children tomorrow. I do not need to see him, but at least the winds in my home will stay calm, and I can work or rest in peace as I like."

Was this a good time to tell Mammi? Elisabeth's revelation could not make the situation any worse.

"Actually," she said, "I've asked Georg to teach me how to drive a wagon." Mammi and Omama looked a little surprised, but Elisabeth continued. "I just need Georg to ride with me one more day, and then I can drive Luki and

Anna to school. If Stefan can bring them home on the days I must help in the fields then everyone is taken care of until Anna can walk again."

Elisabeth didn't have the courage to watch Mammi and Omama's expressions—like all mothers and daughters, they sometimes 'talked' to each other just by exchanging special looks. Elisabeth didn't want any hints about their silent conversation: what if they disapproved of her idea? Only after a few moments did Mammi speak.

"Very well," she said. "I suppose if people are going to gossip about us, at least it's because we're helping ourselves more. Let's go inside. Lissika, bring food in from the cellar. We're all hungry."

As they walked toward the house, Elisabeth dared to ask Mammi about selling some of their animals.

Instead of dismissing her daughter's idea, Mammi listened.

CHAPTER THIRTEEN

Back in bed, Juliana cried. Mom stuck a thermometer in Juliana's ear and waited for the beep.

"You don't have a temperature. Did you eat something at school today? Or here? I do my best to keep the fridge clean and make sure everything's fresh…"

Juliana shook her head. "I didn't throw up. I just felt like I had to. And now I feel like I'm doing a bunch of chaîné turns despite lying in my bed."

Juliana had read the other night that cancer caused nausea. Or maybe it had something to do with her period? Or a heart attack? She'd heard about teens who'd collapsed on the playing field and were dead by the time the paramedics arrived. Was she going to die?

Mom touched Juliana's forehead and cheeks. "You're

flushed, but the thermometer says you're fine. Let me check again." After the thermometer beeped, Mom shook her head. "Nope, nothing."

Juliana rolled to the other side of her bed, stretched out her legs, and pulled them back up. Her body wanted to move, but her stomach wanted her to stay still. Moreover, her heart beat faster than Michael Flatley tapped.

"Mom, I think I'm having a heart attack..."

Mom didn't even look at Juliana. "You're not. Have you been studying too much? Maybe I'm pushing you too hard."

Juliana shook her head. Since when did studying cause this kind of reaction in her?

"What about your marks? Are they bothering you that much?"

Juliana shook her head again, which was the truth. Her marks didn't matter to her anymore. At least not right now.

Silence followed, and Juliana continued to shift around in her bed, trying to keep the nausea at bay but let out her pent-up energy.

"Wait a minute..." Mom said. "You said yesterday you were studying quietly. That's not like you. And you haven't recited random facts for tests or mid-terms for a while. I've seen you spend more time with Tata, which is beautiful—I truly couldn't have hoped for anything better. But you're still not focused on your schoolwork, are you? Are you stressed? Being bullied? Fighting with your friends?"

Juliana shook her head. "Everything at school's going fine..." she said.

Without saying a word, Mom pulled out her phone and began dialling.

Of course. I'm sick as a dog and she calls work, Juliana thought.

"Peter? Hey, it's Katy. I hope you haven't gone to bed yet?...Good. I won't keep you long."

Why would Mom call Uncle Peter at a time like this?

"Listen, I need to ask you something." Mom stepped outside Juliana's room and closed the door. But the doors being paper thin meant Juliana heard everything Mom said. "Back then, until you saw that kiss in that baseball movie...? Yeah, that one."

Baseball movie? How did that relate to Juliana?

"You'd been getting sick a lot, right?...Was it because of...?"

Why was Uncle Peter sick a lot? She kept listening.

"Okay. And did it come suddenly or build up?...Yeah... No, I think it's something else. Her generation is different. Well, for most kids. Immigrants' kids can still have it pretty hard—you know the drill..."

Immigrants' kids? Juliana's generation? Nothing Mom said triggered any kind of idea in Juliana's mind. Mom and Uncle Peter might as well have been speaking a foreign language.

"No, she's not telling me something, but I don't think it's

that...Okay...Thanks so much, Peter. You're okay that I asked?...Thank you. I'm sure she'll be fine, but I don't want to make the same mistake Modr and Tata did with you."

What mistake had Oma and Opa made with Uncle Peter?

"Sorry to keep you, but I had to call. She's never had this before, and...thank you. Enjoy your baguettes and lattes. We'll see you on Sunday. Hopefully you won't be too jet-lagged."

At least I understood the last part, Juliana thought. *Uncle Peter's in France*. Now Juliana felt guilty for assuming Mom was calling work when the call had something to do with her.

Mom came back in, her phone already tucked in her jeans pocket.

"Sometimes I really believe I don't deserve Peter as a brother," she said. "He's so open and loving." She shook her head and changed the topic. "Don't worry, you're not having a heart attack. It's a panic attack."

Juliana had learned about panic attacks before and had even read about them the other day. How could this be a panic attack? She got angry and frustrated and sad, like anyone, but no one in her family had died, or was taking drugs, or anything like that.

"You're really stressed, Jules," Mom said, her voice full of concern. "Uncle Peter got sick often the way you are right now—no fever but nauseous, heart racing. In hindsight, I think some of his stomach bugs were actually this. I even remember him crying some nights, but I was too angry with Tata or Modr for something or other to—" Mom sighed—"to care and ask what was wrong."

"What *was* wrong?" Juliana's curiosity was getting the better of her.

Mom shook her head. "It's not important anymore. But you like to dance your stress out, and you haven't been able to. Tata has been watching you, and you haven't been able to get that private time to be alone with your feelings and your dancing." Mom studied Juliana for a moment. "But whatever's bothering you, it's bigger than what you've ever dealt with before, even bigger than this move. Sweetheart, can you tell me, please? I want to help. Have I pushed you too hard? But I know you'll be so upset with yourself if your marks continue to slip. I'm your mother. Can you please tell me what's bothering you this much?"

Juliana wanted to tell Mom...somehow...but her nausea came back. She bolted off her bed and to the bathroom again.

JULIANA'S HEAD ACHED AND HER STOMACH MUSCLES HURT. She lurched onto her bed and rolled on to her side.

"Here," Mom said, passing the phone to Juliana. "It's

Dad. I thought maybe you were still angry with me from the last couple of weeks and might want to speak to him."

Juliana had never felt so guilty before in her life: Yes, she had been furious a few weeks ago with Mom because of other stuff, but that had nothing to do with her problems now. But she couldn't tell her the real reason either!

"I'll be in the kitchen watching TV," Mom said, and left Juliana alone.

"Jules?" Dad asked.

"Yeah." Juliana's voice croaked.

"Oh, God, you do sound bad. Kiddo, what's going on? I'm at a truck stop, so you have my full attention."

It was now or spend the rest of the evening running to the bathroom. She swallowed hard. She described the man in the long-term care facility again and the smells and how the man and Opa somehow had merged in her mind into one person.

"We started talking about this earlier and then I made us hang up," Dad said. "I shouldn't have. I'm so sorry, Jules. Keep talking. You saw a man who appeared paralyzed..."

Juliana repeated her description, not because she assumed Dad hadn't heard it the first time, but because her mind now wouldn't let go of the image. She didn't know how often she'd repeated it when Dad interrupted her.

"Jules, hold on, just stop." Dad's voice was caring and kind, not impatient. "You're worrying about things that may not even happen."

"I know," Juliana said through her tears. "But I can't stop. I want to study—I want my marks back, I do! But I can't keep my mind on my books. And then Jasmine said to spend as much time with Opa as I can, and Meghan at school has told me I can only dance when I'm young, and what Jasmine told me at the studio, and then Opa said Elisabeth only went to grade six, and Elisabeth studied really hard, and Karl was on TV about cancer and factories and —"

"Whoa...stop again. I think I understand: you can't piece together everything everyone's telling you, and it's leaving you scared about Opa."

Juliana blew her nose and wiped her eyes. "Yeah." To her surprise, her stomach began to settle. Was stress this bad? She had learned stress management techniques in health class, but she never guessed she'd need them: she used dance. She remembered now that her health teacher had talked about breathing, so she took a deep breath and let it out. She risked a sip of water from the water bottle in her dance bag. The coolness of the liquid spread through her body, relaxing her muscles just a little. She took another sip.

"Jules? You there?"

"Yeah, just drinking some water."

Dad let out a sigh of relief. "Good. You worried me for a sec. Let's start at the beginning. Some people need extra help when they get old, so they stay in nursing homes. The people who work in those homes go to college for a year—they're called personal support workers, PSWs for short. Nurses who work there go to university first, I think. Trust me, most of them aren't in it for the money. Most homes aren't horrible places, but it can look that way because of the condition of those people, which is usually no fault of the PSWs."

"But why didn't that man move?"

"It's hard to say. Maybe he had a stroke and his dementia keeps him from learning how to use only one side of his body."

"Couldn't he go to physio? That's what I did with my ankle and wrist."

Dad let out a gentle laugh, which made Juliana feel stupid. She hadn't tried to be funny. Why did adults do that sometimes? "If only it were that simple. But when you have any kind of dementia at such an advanced stage, you can't learn anymore, and in order to do physio well, you need to be able to learn."

"Can't they force him?"

"That would probably be seen as elder abuse, and chances are he's so far gone he wouldn't even react to what anyone would show him."

"So, Opa will someday...?"

"Jules, listen to me. You have to stop dwelling on Opa's future and focus instead on the present. We can slow things down a bit—"

"What do you mean?" Dad's statement was the most hopeful thing Juliana had heard in days.

"We can slow down his Alzheimer's by talking to him, laughing with him, making sure he has healthy food...you know, less trucker food..." Dad's little joke made Juliana smile. "Your Opa likes people...no, he *loves* people. If he had to spend the next few years at home by himself, his mind would probably go much faster."

"So, we can keep his mind going?" Juliana's stomach calmed down even more now.

But caution in Dad's voice deflated her happiness. "It will always be downhill from here. I know that's not what you wanted to hear, Jules, but we can't stop it."

"Oh."

"I'm sorry you're only getting to know him now. Your mom and I failed at that. But with us moving in, Opa's downhill will hopefully be a gentle slope instead of a cliff. I can't give you any guarantees, but we're family and that's why we came: to try to help him."

Juliana's stomach tightened again and her next question flew out. "But what if he gets cancer?" She took in a deep breath—like she'd learned in school—and released it. Her stomach relaxed.

Dad sighed. "Juliana, we can't know what's going to happen to each of us. When you slipped on stage a few years ago, your mom and I really worried you wouldn't be able to dance again. Even back then we saw how important dance had become for you. And here you are, doing amazing."

"Yeah, but that's different. I'm younger and will never work in a rubber factory."

"Why are you talking about the rubber factory?"

Juliana filled him in about the news report.

"That's too bad," Dad said. "But we could talk about what-ifs for hours. If you become a professional dancer, you could injure yourself enough that you'd never be able to dance again. I heard a report on the radio once that some professional athletes get cancer precisely because they push their bodies too hard—what if that happened? We just don't know. One thing I know for sure, though, is this: do you remember the other week, when Opa said he and Oma had come here to build a better life for his family?"

"Yeah. Something about comm...comm..." Juliana always forgot the word Opa used.

"Communism."

"Yeah. What is that?"

"A different discussion. But my point is, Opa came here for you. He didn't know if you would ever exist. Or Aunt Anne's kids. But I'm sure he hoped you all would. What would make him sad is to know that you're sad for his future, when he wants to be happy about yours."

He wants to be happy about my future, she thought. *If Opa and Oma hadn't come here, I wouldn't be here.* Her legs relaxed and her stomach settled.

"He cares about your happiness and that his stories will be remembered by someone," Dad said. "And he's certainly found an eager ear in you."

Not all of Juliana's worries disappeared, but their intensity diminished. *Maybe reminding myself once in a while that Opa wants me to be happy might help*, she thought. *It certainly did now.*

"Jules? You okay? I can't see what's going through your head right now. That's why I wanted to wait until tomorrow, but I didn't realize how badly you needed to talk. I'm really sorry."

"That's okay. Yeah...I'm just thinking..."

"Listen, take it from someone who lost both his parents in their forties. I know Opa has his moods, and they can get worse, or maybe he'll be really happy most of the time as his mind fades. We don't know. But you have him right now. And, I have to say, I'm glad you quit the dance club."

"Yeah. I don't want to go back into one of those homes. Not right now, anyway."

"I'm sorry to hear the experience was so hard on you, but please don't let it scare you. We really don't know what Opa's future holds for him." He paused. "How are you feeling now?"

"I guess I'm still worried, but I feel calmer." Juliana still needed to talk about her studying, but the longer she talked to Dad, the later he might be tomorrow. *My marks have been bad all semester*, she thought. *What's one more day?*

"I think I'm actually good. Well, better. Not perfect, but better. I really don't mind if we talk more tomorrow."

Dad's engine rumbled in the background as he started it up. "Good. I'm going to get going so I can be home as early as possible tomorrow, and I plan to give you a big hug. For now, concentrate on your competition dances and your schooling and spend time with Opa and your new family here." The engine rumbled louder as Dad pushed on the gas. Juliana remembered those sounds from when she used to drive with him in grade school, back in Calgary. "And your new friends. They all seem nice and like they're trying to help you."

"They are," she admitted, smiling. She had found good friends in Kitchener.

"But one last question before I let you go. Do you want me to tell Mom about our conversations—because I need for her to know—or do you want to?"

Juliana worried Mom would start crying in front of her if she talked to her about this. Mom had cried a few weeks before when Opa told everyone why he and Oma had immigrated to Canada in the first place. Mom's crying had made Juliana uncomfortable: parents weren't supposed to cry.

"You can. I want to ask Opa about a drawing."

"Okay. Pass me back to her. But you sound like you're feeling better."

"I am. Thank you."

"You're welcome, sweetie."

Juliana grabbed Elisabeth's book out of her night-table drawer. When Juliana entered the kitchen, she smiled. "Thank you," she said as she passed the phone to Mom, who looked somewhat surprised at Juliana.

"Opa!" she called down the stairs. "I want to ask you something!"

CHAPTER FOURTEEN

"Georg, you're staring like a cow!" Konrad-Bátschi shouted in the back room. All the men, save for Stefan, laughed along with Elisabeth's uncle. Georg, though, didn't appear to notice: he was staring at something far away, something that was likely playing itself in his mind. Had the events from Friday made Georg's nightmares worse? Elisabeth prayed that they would not overwhelm him. If he began to act those terrible dreams out while sitting between two men at a table in a small room, people could get hurt and Georg would suffer more ridicule and humiliation.

If that did happen, Elisabeth wouldn't be able to help: she was sitting in the front room of Konrad-Bátschi's and Margarethe-Néni's house, along with her cousins Susi and Gretche, Eva, two unmarried friends of Susi's, and Maria. It was a typical evening of *majen*. Mammi had encouraged Elisabeth to go out, and despite her disdain for most of Georg's family, Elisabeth enjoyed Eva's company and hoped she'd be able to spend some time with Stefan and Georg. She was pleased that, unexpectedly, Margarethe-Néni had invited Maria, too.

Margarethe-Néni sat at one end of the table to show the women a stitch. Right now, however, they were staring past the kitchen and into the back room, where Georg sat in plain sight of the door.

"A cow in front of an open gate!" Schubkegel Adam, Susi's husband, added. The men, save again for Stefan, roared with laughter. Stefan and Elisabeth exchanged looks. She began to stand up, but Stefan shook his head. He tapped Georg's arm. Georg did not move his eyes but his arm elbowed Stefan, causing him to bump into Adam next to him.

The men laughed again.

"Honestly, Stefan, I don't understand what you see in my brother-in-law," Adam said. "He's as daft as a donkey."

"He's a good man," Stefan replied as he straightened his shirt. "If you took time to get to know him—"

"I don't need to get to know a crazy man. *I* came back from the war and *I'm* not crazy."

The other men nodded in agreement.

"You also didn't fight for three years and lose a wife and child while you were gone."

No one countered Stefan's response. The lack of sympathy for Georg, who remained still in his chair, his eyes unfocused, hurt Elisabeth's heart.

"Don't they put men like him away?" Wagner Michael, Gretche's husband, asked the others. "Arad must have an asylum." He tapped his cigarette into a bowl.

"There are hundreds of thousands of men like him," Stefan said. "Maybe millions. I've seen them begging on the streets in other countries."

"If they can beg on the streets, they can carry a tool," Michael replied.

"And who will pay them?" Stefan asked.

"When God grants their prayers and removes the devil from their soul, then they can work like normal people and get paid."

Elisabeth's hands froze. Did Michael really believe that? *Of course he does*, she thought. *They all do. Even Pastor Fröhlich.*

"Enough about my waste of a son," Konrad-Bátschi said. "It doesn't matter if other men are like him. He's useless to his family. Adam, deal the cards." The men picked up the cards as Adam dealt. As a card slid to Georg, Konrad-Bátschi said, "Leave him out. He couldn't play if you told him what move to make."

The men in Georg's family slapped their hands on the table and laughed.

Stefan shrugged at Elisabeth, signalling to her that they

couldn't help. Georg would have to come out of his other world in his own time. Elisabeth sent a quick prayer to Jesus to help Georg and hoped that he was lost enough that he hadn't heard the taunting from his own family.

Margarethe-Néni closed the door. "The men are too loud," she stated, but a fleeting look of sadness on her face told Elisabeth that her aunt closed the door for a different reason. Did the men's comments about Georg make her sad? That didn't seem possible. Margarethe-Néni hated her son as much as Konrad-Bátschi did. Elisabeth had even seen her slap him during one of his fits. From what Eva had told her, both of his parents punished him like a little boy.

Margarethe-Néni continued with her demonstration, all the young women's eyes on her hands as she stitched a butterfly on the edge of a shawl she was embroidering.

"Georg needs to stop embarrassing us," Susi said as the women resumed their work. "I almost couldn't find a husband because of him." Her two friends nodded sympathetically.

"Michael almost didn't marry me once he saw Georg after the war," Gretche added.

"Really?" one of Susi's friends asked.

Gretche looked up, her face earnest. "Georg had returned at Christmas that year—he didn't have to fight in the Hungarian-Romanian War afterwards. You should have seen him: screaming at no one, thrashing at night in his bed...the devil possessed him. *Every day.*"

Gretche looked like she was enjoying the attention she got about sharing details about her brother.

Elisabeth's stomach churned. She dropped her work on the table in anger. "Do you know what he saw?"

Gretche shrugged. "Why does it matter? Other men have come home and are fine. Adam's normal."

"Did you not hear what Stefan said? That Adam didn't also lose his young family while he was on the front?"

Now Margarethe-Néni spoke up, her voice unusually soft, her eyes cast down. "Everyone thought it best not to tell him." She turned her head in the direction of the door, and the boisterous laughter of the men shot through, along with several calls of Georg's name.

"See?" Gretche said. "It's embarrassing to have a brother like that. Michael asked me just a few days before we got married if I would give birth to children like him."

Susi's eyes opened wide and her friends gasped. "You never told me that," she said. "What did you say?"

Gretche pushed her needle into the fabric and pulled it through the bottom. "That I follow the Word of the Lord, so our children will be normal. He agreed with me and we married. Eva, I really don't understand what made you marry him."

Elisabeth reached over to Eva and grasped her hand. Eva squeezed it back. Eva had married Georg because the parents on both sides had convinced her she would lead a comfortable life, especially once he inherited his father's blacksmithing shop. Only through Elisabeth had Eva eventually understood that these fits controlled Georg, not the other way around.

Margarethe-Néni interrupted the conversation. "Gretche, you have your father's hands. That looks like an ugly beetle. Susi, yours looks like a mosquito. Take out those stitches."

Her daughters protested, but Margarete-Néni insisted.

Elisabeth, Maria, and Eva made eye contact with one another. Although Maria still disagreed a little with Elisabeth that the war had caused Georg's fits and nightmares, she understood that Elisabeth cared. To Eva, Elisabeth had become a friend who had helped her see her husband's world through his eyes.

"You two are as slow as turtles," Margarethe-Néni said to her daughters.

If her aunt was sad, she didn't show it. In fact, she was as angry as Mammi...

But Mammi gets angry when she's sad, Elisabeth realized. *Was Margarethe-Néni the same?*

"Frau Schuhmacher," Maria said, "I'm having some difficulty with the wings." She showed her handiwork to Margarethe-Néni who waved it away. "Your work is fine," she said.

Elisabeth mouthed "thank you" to her friend for trying to lift the mood.

"I went to the store to buy some yeast and saw Wagner

Anni. Her dress was too short. Did anyone else see it today?" Gretche asked everyone at the table. To Elisabeth's dismay, Gretche's rude comment instead of Maria's polite question relieved the tension in the room.

Elisabeth had come here to avoid Mammi's family, believing an evening in this household would be better. *I guess I was wrong*, she thought.

Susi raised her chin. "I saw it when I went to help at the church today. I'm certain she tried to hide behind the pews while she was dusting them so no one would notice."

Gretche and Eva chuckled at Susi's comment.

"Maybe she hasn't had time to lengthen it," Elisabeth offered in Wagner Anni's defense. The poor girl, who had also received confirmation with Elisabeth, was often the topic of gossip for her appearance, especially her crooked nose.

"I'm certain she has other dresses," Gretche said. "Her dress looked fine at the market on Tuesday. Her nose, though..."

More laughter.

"Maybe she's trying to be more modern," Maria added with a little pride. "I cut my bangs because it's the fashion now, and the skirts in America are much shorter than ours."

Elisabeth envied Maria for her courage at cutting her bangs against tradition. Maria's grandmother's cousin had sent Maria a fashion magazine from America a couple of months ago, and she and Elisabeth had by now memorized most of it. Elisabeth hoped Mammi would someday be able to make shoes like the ones in the magazine, but Mammi would need new lasts—wooden forms to make the shoes on—to create shoes with a fashionable heel.

Gretche gave Maria a look. "There is no reason why a girl like her should be in the village with a dress that's at least five centimetres too short. She has no husband to care for."

"She may not get one," Eva added, tapping herself on the nose. But as everyone laughed again, she glanced apologetically at Elisabeth. Elisabeth tried not to be disappointed in Georg's wife—she lived in this household, with Konrad-Bátschi and Margarethe-Néni, and witnessed daily how they belittled her husband. Elisabeth hadn't liked Eva when they had met about a year ago at their wedding, but this year, Elisabeth had learned that Eva had to behave a certain way just to survive here. It was also the reason she hadn't defended her husband before.

"Susi, get everyone more tea and coffee," Margarethe-Néni said.

Susi opened the door to the kitchen, and Elisabeth followed her with her gaze and looked into the back room. The men were arguing about recent news and events during their card game. Georg had come out of his spell but he just stared at his lap. Elisabeth caught Stefan's gaze and then he leaned over to Georg and whispered something. Georg looked up and made eye contact with Elisabeth but his face remained otherwise expressionless.

Gossip in the front room continued—this time about someone Gretche knew through her husband's family—and Elisabeth chose not to say anything. She again glanced into the back room where Stefan was now helping Georg up and around the table, likely to get some fresh air. Elisabeth's eyes were mysteriously drawn to Stefan.

Stefan smiled at Elisabeth as he opened the house door for Georg. She blushed, returned the smile, and then continued with her handiwork. Maria and Eva both nudged her, mischievous grins lighting up their faces, and Elisabeth blushed even more.

"How is Georg doing?" Elisabeth asked Eva as they exited the church. "I was really worried about him the other night at your home."

They stepped down the stairs outside the small, yellow building and walked together to the churchyard.

Eva adjusted the knot of her dark blue headscarf. "Thank you for standing up for him," she said. She stared at the ground. "I'm fearful of his family, but I feel ashamed when they speak so of him."

Elisabeth slipped her arm under Eva's and led her to a

quiet corner in the churchyard. "It can't be easy living there."

Eva shook her head. "I envy all his siblings, but Samuel most of all, because he can live out on the *salasch*. If Georg and I could live there, my husband would have fewer nightmares and fits. I'm certain of it."

Elisabeth agreed with Eva: Georg did often appear more at ease riding a horse and working the land, away from prying eyes.

"But now, he's slipping away more," Eva said. "He even sleeps in the workshop so he doesn't wake us up with his nightmares."

Elisabeth glanced down at Eva's growing belly and wondered if the baby they were expecting was causing this.

"Yes, I think he worries about the baby and me," Eva said, answering Elisabeth's silent question.

"And now with Mammi..." Elisabeth didn't finish her sentence: they both understood what she meant.

Eva nodded. "But she does look like she's feeling better. Will she be at the dance this afternoon?" The slight change in Eva's voice suggested to Elisabeth that she wanted to speak about something else.

Elisabeth shook her head. "She said she'll be sad that she won't be at my first dance, but the doctor told her not to work too much, and she wants to spend a full day in the workshop tomorrow. She said if she has no orders, she'll at least clean it up and show Luki something new."

"That's wonderful," Eva said, though her voice didn't sound happy.

"Rosina! Wait up!" Anna called through the churchyard as she hurried on her crutches to catch up to her younger sister.

"You're too slow!" Rosina shouted back, teasing.

Elisabeth and Eva smiled. "They really must be quieter," Elisabeth said. "Maybe I should go and speak with them."

"Let them be," Eva said. Elisabeth was certain she caught Eva glancing disdainfully toward her mother-in-law across the yard. "They're children and deserve to keep their innocent happiness a little longer."

Elisabeth agreed and the two reached a quiet corner where they could talk without anyone listening. Georg and Stefan joined them a few moments later.

"Thank you for showing me how to drive our wagon," Elisabeth said to Georg.

He nodded. "Stefan said you drove it on Friday without any difficulties."

"I loved taking Anna and Luki by myself! People stared at me, and they even stared at me today in church. But to not have to ask you to stop your duties to help my family with something so simple...it's so very nice." A guilty smile crept onto Elisabeth's face. "It's also fun."

Stefan smiled at Elisabeth. "So, what's next for you? A bicycle?"

"Mammi's heart would stop if I did that!"

All four laughed, and Elisabeth thanked God for the change in mood.

"Elisabeth!"

She turned around and saw Mammi, dressed in black from head to toe except for her striped socks, walking up to them. The happiness in the group disappeared. Had Mammi heard Elisabeth's joke? Elisabeth asked Jesus for forgiveness and then tried to think of why else Mammi wanted to speak with her. Mammi didn't like it when Elisabeth spent time with Georg, but Mammi hadn't actually pulled Elisabeth away from him in a while. So, what did Mammi want to say to her? Were Elisabeth's white blouse and skirt dirty? She inspected her clothing: no. Her hands and shawl? They were also clean. Elisabeth tightened her white headscarf. She couldn't find anything wrong with her appearance. So why was Mammi calling her?

The circle split open to allow Mammi to join them.

"Frau Schuhmacher," Stefan said, tipping his cap.

"Lissa-Néni," Georg and Eva said, each nodding.

Mammi nodded at each one in return—including Georg. Elisabeth's skin tingled: Mammi neither asked her to leave the group nor ignored Georg. This had never happened before.

Then Mammi faced Georg. "Lissika has spoken with me about our animals: we do not need all of them, and caring for them is too much work for our family this year."

"Elisabeth has told me so, too," Georg said.

"Good. Then you know what I'm talking about. Will you and Samuel take care of all our pigs, all but one of our cows, and our second horse? Samuel and Deaf-Lissi may sell whatever the animals produce at the market—so long as we have two pigs for slaughter in the fall—and use the second horse as needed. But I expect to have the animals back when Lukas returns. Lissika will occasionally walk our cow out to the *salasch* and bring home a different one, and she can help with the animals when she is out there if needed."

Elisabeth and Eva exchanged looks: had the devil possessed Mammi that she spoke so freely to Georg?

"I'll speak with Samuel on Tuesday," Georg said, "but I'm certain he'll agree. Thank you, Lissa-Néni."

Mammi nodded. "I want to be clear on one point: do not for one moment believe that I have forgiven you. But I cannot ignore what I have seen. You have helped my family very much, and without complaint. Thank you."

Without waiting for Georg to respond, Mammi turned around and left to join a group of her own friends.

Elisabeth exchanged glances with Stefan and Eva. Mammi always spoke directly, sometimes without regard for another person's feelings. But she also never offered empty compliments. Her thank you to Georg was genuine.

"I'm sorry about Mammi's comments," Elisabeth said, wanting to at least apologize for Mammi's rude words.

But Georg shook his head and squeezed his eyes shut, trying in vain to prevent tears from falling. Eva, Stefan, and Elisabeth closed in around him to protect him from nosy gossips. Eva leaned her head on his upper arm, while Elisabeth pulled a handkerchief out of her hand purse and offered it to Georg.

In a voice barely above a whisper, Georg said, "She said 'thank you.'"

CHAPTER FIFTEEN

"Opa, why would Elisa—Omama —draw a cracked egg? Was she angry or something?" Juliana asked, holding Elisabeth's book open. She called her "Omama" to others, because that seemed like the right thing to do.

Opa laughed. "No, Yulika, not at all. This is an Easter egg."

An Easter egg? There were no decorations on the shell but instead cracks spread from the tip to about half way. Juliana shared her confusion with Opa, and he laughed again. His laugh was friendly, though, and not mocking.

"The last time you asked me about her drawings, they were from her confirmation. Confirmation always happened on Palm Sunday. So this has to be an Easter egg. They didn't use fancy colours and stickers like you do here," he explained. "They boiled the eggs with onion peels to make brown eggs."

"Brown? Brown Easter eggs?" Brown reminded Juliana of mud in the spring, not colourful flowers and green leaves.

Laughing again, but this time with a shrug, Opa said, "They used what they had." He patted her on the knee. "But you don't have to worry. They also used chamomile to make yellow ones..." His voice trailed off and Juliana worried he would begin hallucinating again. She took a deep breath to prepare herself, but he shook his head. "I don't remember what else they used. When we coloured eggs here with Annie, we did what other Canadians did. We bought...what are they called? Those boxes with every-thing in them..."

"Egg-colouring kits?"

"*Ja, genau.* Kits. We bought kits."

Opa lost his smile, as though the memory attached to it had vanished. Juliana needed to bring him out of whatever made him sad. "But you haven't told me why the egg is cracked," she said, holding the book up in front of his face. Opa's smile returned.

"We called it *titschen*," he said, beaming. He raised a hand to shoulder level and pretended to hold an egg in it. "You did this to another person's egg." He pretended to tap his egg against another one. "If your egg didn't crack, you won."

Juliana broke out into giggles. "Seriously? You boiled and coloured eggs and then cracked them?"

Opa furrowed his eyebrows and Juliana worried her reaction had insulted him. "But you colour them and then eat them," he said. "How is that fun?"

Juliana admitted he had a point. "So this drawing doesn't mean Omama felt like an egg that was about to crack? Like she was feeling stressed?" That's what the drawing said to Juliana.

Opa shook his head. "You read in the newspaper all about stress. Everyone today is stressed. But we didn't have that word. We were sad or angry or frustrated, not stressed." He began turning the pages in his mother's book of drawings and Juliana tried not to look at the ones she hadn't seen yet. "I think you found a funeral in here…" He stopped when he found the page Juliana and Dad had once discussed.

In the drawing lay a man in a plain, thin coffin. This wasn't Susanna Schubkegel, of course, but the coffin and arrangement of flowers matched those in the photograph. Behind the man in the coffin stood nine people, their hands folded in prayer.

Opa pointed to a large man standing beside a smaller woman. "This is Georg, Mammi's cousin. He was useless to his family."

Opa had said these exact words several times over the past few months about this Georg. Juliana had researched a little online herself and guessed this cousin must have suffered from post-traumatic stress disorder after fighting in World War I. Juliana had tried to explain this to Opa, but he had refused to listen. *What would he think of panic attacks?* she wondered. He either didn't let on that he knew she'd experienced one, or he'd already forgotten.

Interrupting her thoughts, Opa continued, pointing to the small woman. "This is his wife, Eva. A very kind woman but very sad. She could never remarry. Ah!" He pointed to the next row of people. "These are Mammi's siblings: Luki-Bátschi, Anni-Néni, and Rosi-Néni. 'Néni' for 'aunt,' and 'bátschi' for 'uncle.'"

Opa had shown her these people before. His mind seemed to be in a good space right now, so Juliana pressed for more information. "Did you know them?"

"Only Anni-Néni."

Anni-Naney. That's what Juliana would be calling her Aunt Anne if they all lived in Romania right now.

"Romanian sounds like a nice language," she said, only for Opa to laugh again. It irritated her like Dad's laughter had earlier. She was trying to say something nice. Why did it make Opa laugh?

"Those words are Hungarian," Opa said. "Even though a lot of Romanians lived in the village when I was a boy, it belonged to Hungary when our ancestors arrived. They came from a town called Mezöberény. I don't know where they came from in Germany. They had Hungarian words in their German. But your *oma* had Romanian words in hers. Our children always laughed at us because some of the words sound funny in English."

He returned his gaze to the drawing. "But when everyone was sad, like at a funeral, Mammi used to say at least they stopped fighting with each other."

"Did they fight a lot? It doesn't sound like a friendly place when you say that."

Opa looked taken aback. "Oh, no, Yulika! Semlak was very friendly. But people said what they were thinking, and that sometimes made people angry. Still, you knew where everyone stood. Not like here. You don't know if someone is being nice or if they want something from you."

Juliana had to agree with Opa. As angry as Jasmine's comments about the paralyzed man had made her, she had to admit that Jasmine was right: there really was nothing Juliana could do about Opa's disease. She'd make sure to call Jasmine on the weekend and say so.

Opa closed the book and handed it back to Juliana. "I need to tell your mother to boil eggs for Sunday. We should do this Easter tradition. It will be fun! Especially because it's my family birthday party!" With a burst of energy Juliana had come accept as normal for Opa whenever he suddenly remembered he had to do something, he jumped up from his bed and shuffled out the door. "I can't forget!" he shouted back as he climbed the stairs.

A KNOCK ON JULIANA'S BEDROOM DOOR AND MOM ENTERED, a 'mom smile' on her face. "You're looking much better," she said.

Stretching on the floor, Juliana nodded. "I didn't get what was happening to me."

Mom sat on the edge of Juliana's bed. "Once I realized that Peter had had those same symptoms for so long, I wanted to call him and ask to make sure."

"What was causing him all that stress?"

"It's not my story to tell, Jules."

Juliana recalled Mom's side of her conversation with her brother. She'd talked about Juliana's generation being different, immigrant kids still having a hard time, and Uncle Peter 'knowing the drill.' Juliana also remembered when she and Sophie had found Elisabeth's letter tucked inside an old encyclopedia and how Uncle Peter could read the old script in those books. When Juliana had asked how, he said Oma had made him read the Bible, expecting him to change.

A light bulb went off in Juliana's head. "Opa and Oma expected Uncle Peter to be straight, didn't they?"

Mom looked in the other direction as she nodded. "I should've gone elsewhere in the house to call him. I guess I was panicking a little and not thinking clearly."

Juliana sat up on the floor. "But why is this still a secret?

My middle name was a secret, that Dad's parents died in their forties was a secret...why all these secrets? Why won't you tell me these things? I'm almost fifteen."

Mom inspected her hands and said nothing for a few moments. Juliana was tired of all these secrets. Nothing so far had shocked her or hurt her in any way. In fact, the more she learned about her family, the better she understood them, not to mention the friend she had found in her great-grandmother. Why wouldn't her parents tell her these things?

"Mom, I'm old enough."

Mom nodded. "I guess once you decide not to tell someone something, you don't know when to actually tell them." She made eye contact with Juliana and Juliana stopped stretching and sat next to Mom on her bed. "Dad will talk to you about his family when he's ready to. But when Annie and Peter and I were talking about us moving back home—well, to my home—Peter asked us not to tell you about his coming out."

"But I know he's gay...what's the big deal?"

Mom shook her head. "He didn't want you to think less of Opa. But we probably should talk about this now, because who knows if an old memory replays itself inside Opa's mind. The last thing any of us wants is for you to not like Opa because of old beliefs."

Juliana never understood why some parents didn't love their gay and lesbian children, and to learn that Opa and

Oma didn't like their son for a time disappointed her. So far, Opa's anger—whenever Juliana saw it—focused on Mom leaving for Calgary and not coming home. He had never mentioned Uncle Peter. *But I suppose that could change, right?* she thought. Learning during one of his anger spells that he didn't like Uncle Peter because of his sexual orientation would have hurt Juliana, too.

Mom seemed to read her mind. "Tata loves Peter now. They resolved their issues and Tata and Modr realized they were wrong. You have to remember, they came from a different country, and although Modr grew up in the city, she still had old beliefs. Tata grew up in Semlak, where people were trying to hold on to the threads of their lives after World War Two. Peter hoped you would get to know and love Opa for who he is today, not who he was fifteen or twenty years ago."

Juliana recalled what she'd said about Opa when she was still in Calgary and then a few days later, in the car. She told Mom so, and Mom stroked her daughter's hair.

"I guess I wouldn't want Opa to think badly of me because I said those things," Juliana said.

"I'll be honest: it did hurt to hear that. But I knew that wasn't you: You were furious because we had pulled you away from a life you loved."

"Just like it's not Opa when he gets angry sometimes?"

Mom tucked Juliana's hair behind her ears. "I had never thought of it like that. I guess we all get angry from time to time. But as I said, Opa accepts Peter now and has for years. If he says anything mean about him, it's his dementia, not your *opa*. Understood?"

Juliana nodded.

"Now, your name. That we never told you where your middle name came from was my fault." Mom took a deep breath. "Back in Romania, they didn't use middle names. That's a North American thing. Aunt Anne gave her kids middle names from family members, both from her side and your Uncle Phillip's side, and Sophie was named after someone from our side, too." Mom sighed again. "But I was tired of hearing about 'the old country.' We lived in Canada. I wanted you to be your own person and not feel you had to follow in someone else's footsteps. But Modr and Tata caused such a ruckus when I was pregnant with you that I finally caved in. I'm pretty sure I screamed at him to just give me a name, and he said 'Elizabeth.' I knew who she was, although Opa actually rarely talked about his mother—almost everything you're learning is new to me. I said, 'Fine!' and that was that. I wish I could tell you there was something more genuine, more heartfelt behind it."

Juliana wanted to keep talking, but she saw the weariness in Mom's eyes. *At least she's answering some of my questions now*, she thought.

"I'm glad you let him name me," Juliana said, hoping to cheer Mom up a little.

"To be honest, now that I'm learning more about her,

I'm glad Tata forced us to give you her name as your middle name. She sounds like a remarkable person." Mom shrugged. "Who knows? Maybe having footsteps from the past to follow makes walking into the future a little easier."

Juliana stood up and gave Mom a hug. "Thank you, and I'm sorry."

Mom stroked Juliana's hair. "It's all right, sweetie. But remember, you can talk to anyone in my family, okay? I can understand why this time you didn't want to, but..." Mom placed her hand on the doorknob as she collected her thoughts. "We're all worried for Tata's future. And sometimes it helps to talk about your worries with others who worry. But don't say anything to Scott. He's too young." Scott was eight and the youngest of Aunt Anne and Uncle Phillip's six children.

"Sophie?"

Mom nodded. "Sophie would be the best person to talk to, actually. Annie can tell she's scared about Opa, but she won't open up to her. I think it's because Annie's got her hands full with Sophie's therapies and appointments. It would comfort Annie a little to know Sophie has a friend she can confide in."

Juliana nodded.

"Now, get back to your stretching and then get to bed. You've got a long weekend ahead of you. Get some rest, we'll have fun on Sunday—Tata wants me to boil and colour eggs in onion skins—and then we can start fresh on

Monday. I'll make sure to talk to Opa and tell him you sometimes need to practise alone."

Juliana smiled. "Thank you."

Mom closed the door behind her.

Juliana opened Elisabeth's book to the drawing of the cracked egg again.

"If I could erase those cracks, I definitely would," she said, smiling. "But these cracks are your truth. Whatever it was that day, I'm sure they made you happy." She closed the book and hugged it to her chest.

CHAPTER SIXTEEN

"Act like ladies and don't leave with a boy," said Peter-Bátschi to Elisabeth and Little Sophie over a lively polka the seven-piece brass band in the tavern was playing. He headed for the bar.

Elisabeth nodded politely to hide the offense her uncle's comment caused her.

Omama shook her head at her son. "That he would say such a thing to either of you. And look: he already has his first beer."

Mammi had insisted Elisabeth attend her first Sunday afternoon dance with Omama, which meant being accompanied by Peter-Bátschi and arriving with Little Sophie, too. Sophie-Néni stayed home because of pain that sometimes required her to lie down for hours at a time.

The sight of her uncle still angered Elisabeth, especially because he had not apologized for his behaviour last Wednesday. Little Sophie had said not a word along the way to the tavern, which was on the main street, farther down from their church. Elisabeth had hoped to learn what happened once he got home—part of her wished Sophie-Néni had yelled at him, even though Jesus frowned upon such thoughts.

As Elisabeth followed behind her cousin and Omama, the women all stared at her new, perfectly pleated, blue-green cashmere skirt. It reached just below the middle of her shins, and her four white underskirts pushed it out into a beautiful, full shape that would make her look like she was floating on air when she danced. The cotton of her blouse was so thin one could almost see through it. But its thinness would also help keep her cool, and the cotton was easy to clean. Unbeknownst to Elisabeth, Omama had sewn a skirt and blouse each for her and Little Sophie. *That's why she sent me to the* salasch *so often*, Elisabeth thought. *So she had time to sew our new outfits*. Mammi had finished the blouse with all kinds of colourful notions and stitches, including red ribbons sewn along the sleeves. To complete her outfit, Elisabeth wore a white shawl over her shoulders with orange, red, blue-green, and yellow flowers embroidered throughout. That Rosina hadn't said a word all week had at first impressed Elisabeth, until Rosina had begun insisting that she deserved extra cookies yesterday because she'd had to stay home every day with Omama.

She wanted payment for the extra silence, Elisabeth thought. *I would have wanted the same at her age!*

"Do you have your handkerchief?" Omama asked as she led Elisabeth through the tavern to a table with several women sitting around it.

"Yes, I do, Omama," Elisabeth said, and she showed her the handkerchief Anna had embroidered for her confirmation. Little Sophie showed hers, too.

Omama inspected them. "No stains. Lovely work by Anna, Lissika. Little Sophie, you can do better next time. Neither of you can dance without your handkerchief."

Both young women nodded.

"Elisabeth!" A moment later Maria stood in front of her best friend and grabbed both of Elisabeth's hands. "You look positively exquisite!"

Maria liked using fancy words, and Elisabeth enjoyed that about her friend.

Elisabeth blushed. "Look at my shoes." She pushed out a foot.

Little Sophie turned away, but Maria clapped her hands to her cheeks and jumped up and down.

"You look like a monkey," Omama said to her. Both girls tried to refrain from laughing, but small smiles still broke out on their faces. Mammi had said the same thing to them once before, and one glance at Maria told Elisabeth they were thinking the same thing: that they simply enjoyed 'being monkeys' from time to time.

Elisabeth told Maria the happy news, that the shoes Mammi had been embroidering had indeed been meant for Elisabeth.

"They are so beautiful!" Maria exclaimed.

Within moments, others began staring at Elisabeth's black embroidered satin shoes: mothers, grandmothers, and young men.

Omama let out a soft grunt as her gaze flowed around the room. "Luther may be rolling in his grave," she said, "but your *mammi* was right. Lots of boys are staring at you. I may need to pay my daughter to make such shoes for Little Sophie."

It saddened Elisabeth that Mammi wouldn't see the reaction to her shoes, but she would tell her as soon as she returned home this evening.

"You must come show my mother!" Maria said. Omama sat down and waved Elisabeth off. Little Sophie suddenly found herself alone, and Elisabeth hoped her cousin would soon find a friend or acquaintance.

When Elisabeth looked back as Maria dragged her forward, she saw Omama leaning over to several other older women at the table, all of them staring at Elisabeth's shoes. Did they approve of them? Their faces gave her no hint; they looked as stern as always.

"Mammi!" Maria said, pulling Elisabeth's attention back to her.

"Good afternoon, Frau Haibach," Elisabeth said.

"Good afternoon, Lissika." Frau Haibach wore black from head to toe. While young married women like Eva, who had no children, still dressed in colourful skirts and blouses, women of Frau Haibach's age dressed in black, even at dances. It was inappropriate for women with grown children to dress like younger women.

The band finished the song and switched to a waltz. The dancers on the floor joined in, their flowing movements the opposite of the jumpy polka.

"But I'd heard your mother was going to make shoes with heels," Frau Haibach said, a hint of disappointment in her voice.

Without missing a beat, Elisabeth answered, "Mammi said these would be more accepted first, and she can make these right away. She will begin making shoes with heels in the summer."

Mammi had told Elisabeth to give that answer should anyone ask, and it worked: Frau Haibach nodded. "They are indeed lovely, especially for visits to family and friends. Your mother's embroidery is among the finest in the church."

Elisabeth barely contained a squeal at the compliment. "Thank you! I will tell her."

"Tell her, too, that I want a pair for myself and my daughter and will come by tomorrow to order them."

Elisabeth's smile grew, and Maria looked just as excited. "I will!" she replied.

Frau Haibach asked after Mammi's health and Elisabeth answered her questions, also repeating what Mammi had told her to say: that she would be out the following Sunday but would take orders for shoes like Elisabeth's starting tomorrow.

"Lissika!" Omama called as she hobbled up to Elisabeth, a young man in tow. "This is Kaiser Michael, son of Kaiser Johann. You met him on Easter Monday."

Elisabeth pretended to show interest by looking at him more closely. His blond hair was neatly trimmed, his linen shirt was well pressed, and his black boots, which reached to just under his knees, were perfectly polished. But when Elisabeth looked into his brown eyes, she saw something she did not like. Hagel Samuel's eyes—a young man Omama and Mammi had tried to introduce Elisabeth to once—had shown the same quality: the assumption that he was always right. Along with his rudeness about Stefan's arm last week, Elisabeth could say within moments of meeting him a second time that she still did not like him.

The band finished the waltz and paused for a moment as some of the players took a drink before beginning a new one.

"May I have your first dance?" Kaiser Michael asked, extending his hand to her.

Elisabeth would have humiliated her family if she said no, so she accepted. "I have to admit, though, with Tata gone, I haven't been able to learn how to dance."

Kaiser Michael smiled as he raised his chest. "I will show you."

Elisabeth took his hand and he led her to the dance floor, where other couples already dipped and flowed in time with the music.

Kaiser Michael showed Elisabeth the proper arm positions, and the strength of his grip on her back and extended arm surprised her. "One, two, three...Yes, that's right." He guided her around the dance floor, steering her clear of the more advanced couples.

Elisabeth enjoyed the steps but felt badly for her partner: the tight smile on his face told her that her lack of experience frustrated him.

Kaiser Michael tried to ask Elisabeth questions, but she was too focused on her feet to be able to talk at the same time. She apologized several times, but his grip tightened the more frustrated he became.

"I really am sorry," she said. She tripped over his toe and apologized again.

Out of the corner of her eye, she saw Georg standing against a wall, watching her with a slightly amused smile. Next to him stood Stefan, his hand over his mouth, repressing a laugh.

Elisabeth tripped again and hit her forehead against Kaiser Michael's nose.

"Oh no! Are you all right?" she asked in a panic.

Kaiser Michael touched his nose several times to check

for blood, but there was nothing.

Elisabeth's cheeks reddened and her gaze flew over to Omama, who had a scowl on her face.

"I really am sorry. Can I...?"

Without letting her finish, Kaiser Michael held her even tighter and led her around the dance floor. It felt uncomfortable, but if they had stopped, everyone would have gossiped about them for weeks. As much as Elisabeth wanted this first dance to be over, she didn't want Mammi hearing about her oldest daughter's failure by the time Elisabeth got home. Everyone watched the confirmands at their first dance, now that they were allowed to attend.

I'm the only one who doesn't know how to dance, Elisabeth thought. She forced herself to concentrate on her feet so she wouldn't mess up again. She found the three-step rhythm easy, but with the way Kaiser Michael turned them around, she needed to stay focused. Sweat started to drip down her temples. At least her white handkerchief kept Kaiser Michael from feeling the sweat on her palm. When the waltz finished, he looked disappointed. He nodded his head to her and was about to lead her off the floor when a familiar voice spoke from behind them.

"May I have the next dance?"

Elisabeth caught Kaiser Michael's look of disapproval as she turned to face Stefan.

She had never paid much attention to Stefan's attire at church, but suddenly here, in the tavern, his polished boots over his dark linen pants, topped with a linen shirt and black, button-up vest, gave him a distinguished air. Even though he was, for the most part, dressed the same as Kaiser Michael, Stefan looked like the gentleman he was.

The band began a polka, and Elisabeth's cheeks burned as she answered.

"Yes, but I don't know how to polka."

Stefan shrugged. "And I haven't danced since I lost my arm."

They stared at each other, wondering for a moment how to place their hands. Both smiled sheepishly and Elisabeth could feel all the women in the room staring at her. She forced her eyes to keep staring at Stefan, though it didn't require much effort.

"How about we hold hands," she offered, extending her right hand so Stefan could hold it, "and just do whatever works with the other side."

They giggled as Stefan placed his stump under her arm, and she put her hand on his shoulder.

"The polka's easier," he said amidst the loud music. "You just hop and stomp around!" In a beat, he pulled on her hand and pushed with his stump to lead her around the room.

Elisabeth's smile reached from one ear to the other.

CHAPTER SEVENTEEN

Juliana lay on her bed, enjoying the sunlight streaming through her window, her thoughts full of the week's events. She understood now that everyone in the family worried about Opa.

She remembered what Dad had said on the phone, that Opa and Oma had come here to give their future family a better life. "I have a phone, a computer...our floors have carpet." She continued to list in her mind the different things she had that Elisabeth hadn't had: electricity, school past Grade 6, dance classes, cars, the Internet, lots of books...Opa had also told Juliana once that she had freedom and he hadn't. It had to do with Communism. She promised herself to look it up sometime. Meghan and even quiet Shawna at school had joined recent student protests about government cuts to education but politics bored Juliana to tears.

"Elisabeth grew up with her whole family and community," Juliana said out loud. "Her whole life. I will never have that experience. Well, I sort of do now, but I didn't when I first moved here, so I had to make new friends."

But she had managed all of it. She didn't have her marks under control yet, but she had become accustomed to life in Kitchener for the most part, had friends at dance and school, and had found a special friendship with Sophie.

"Actually..." Juliana rolled onto her stomach and reached her hand as far down as possible between the wall and her bed and grasped a ball of paper wedged into a corner. "Got it!"

She rolled onto her back and uncrumpled the ball to reveal a list of the goals she had recorded in January. With all the difficulties of the move, she had torn the page out of its notebook and thrown it at her window. Disposing of it would have made her feel like a failure, so she'd hidden it: out of sight, out of mind.

She reviewed her goals:

✓ *Get my splits*

✓ *Bend my back in half*

✓ *Make and keep 5 new friends in January*

✓ *Maintain 90% average at new school*

✓ *Raise competition average from 85% to 95%*

She smiled. Those goals sounded more like 'Meghan' or 'Jasmine' goals, not 'Juliana' goals. At least not goals for the Juliana she had become over the past few months. These goals seemed pretty naïve, given what she'd since learned about Opa and the Schuhmacher family. She got off her bed, opened up a drawer in her dresser, and dug underneath her sweaters.

"Found you," she said as she pulled out the notebook she'd torn this page from, another artefact she couldn't bear to dispose of. Not only would it have been bad for the environment, using it for something else would have reminded her of her failure to keep these goals.

"But I chose the wrong goals to begin with. That's the problem!" Happy with her discovery, she sat at her desk and pulled out a pen.

✓ *Spend more time with Opa*

✓ *Study for an hour a day after homework*

✓ *Limit dance practice to two hours a day max!*

✓ *Let myself worry sometimes but not for too long*

She reviewed her list. Four goals didn't seem like enough, even though she still struggled with school.

"I need something easy," she said to herself. A moment later, she added this:

✓ *Get my splits*

"Your drawings are your memories," she said to Elisabeth's book. "My book of goals is sort of mine, in a way. This afternoon, I'll write down my plans for achieving these goals." With it being Good Friday, Juliana had the day off school. "But first, I'll catch up on some studying." She closed the book and turned her attention to her open science book. She had a test coming up and wanted to at least try to reach a higher mark.

"I'll go out with Sophie tomorrow," she said before pushing all other thoughts out of her head and beginning to read the first chapter she needed to review.

JULIANA AND SOPHIE ENTERED THE CAFÉ IN BELMONT Village, a shopping strip about a thirty-second walk from both their homes. Juliana loved the café's 1950s vibe, with its pink, black, white, and chrome colour scheme. The tables and chairs had modern, clean, simple lines, providing an orderly contrast to the flair of the '50s. It was exactly Juliana's style.

The girls grabbed a table by the window. The longtime owner of the café, Casimiro, an older Portuguese man with a strip of white hair around the sides and back of his head, came to take their order.

"Root beer float today, Miss Roth?" Casimiro asked in his Portuguese accent, a smile on his face. The last time Sophie and Juliana had been there, Juliana had tried a root beer float for the first time. Only after drinking half the tall glass had she come to enjoy it.

"No," Juliana said with a smile. "We're going to be eating so much sugar tomorrow, I'd rather have a tea. Peppermint?"

"Just like your Uncle Peter," Casimiro said.

"Just like Uncle Peter," Juliana repeated, something else she had learned the last time she and Sophie had come.

"And Miss Morgan?" he asked Sophie.

"A tea, too. It's still chilly outside. But I'd like chamomile."

Casimiro nodded. "Coming right up, and you don't have to pay today. Your grandfather called and said to put your bill on his tab." Casimiro returned to the kitchen, where his wife was wiping down a countertop.

Sophie leaned forward, resting her chin on her hands. "Well, that's really nice of Opa."

Juliana nodded in agreement.

"Mom said you weren't feeling good yesterday," Sophie said. "Everything okay?"

Juliana nodded again.

"Stomach bug?"

How should Juliana answer? Mom had said Juliana should share her worries with Sophie, but what if she shared too much? Sophie had been frightened by Opa's hallucination a few weeks ago, although the counselling she had received alongside Juliana and their mothers later had helped.

Juliana shook her head in answer to Sophie's question.

"On Tuesday, I danced in a nursing home. And I saw this elderly man there who scared me."

Sophie cocked her head to the side. "How?"

"Jasmine wanted to know that, too. She's a friend at my dance studio. This man reminded me of Opa a little, but it was like he was paralyzed, and his mouth hung open. He didn't move at all, just stared into space." She left out the details about the briefs and bib.

"I guess that would creep me out, too," Sophie said.

Juliana twirled her hair on her finger and stared at the table. "I don't want Opa ending up like him. I mean, is Alzheimer's going to eat so much of his brain that he can't move?" She'd read about how Alzheimer's caused the growth of some kind of plaque in the brain and destroyed it over years.

Sophie sighed and stared at the table. Juliana worried she'd said too much.

"After Opa thought we were his mother," Sophie began, "I realized how serious this was. He'd gotten mad at Mom a couple of times before, but I brushed it off as father-daughter stuff. Maybe it wasn't?"

Juliana shrugged and added "I don't know" in case Sophie couldn't see her shrug. "I've seen him angry before, too, and I assumed it was normal, but when he grabbed a stack of clean tea towels from the kitchen and took them to the basement to wash, I knew it was more than that. But this man in the nursing home...what if he was like Opa once? Angry and checked out from reality once in a while? Funny and laughing and full of love the rest of the time? How do you talk about this without sounding rude? Dad said the man could've suffered a stroke. But even still...he looked almost...forgotten in the nursing home. Like no one cared about him."

Casimiro brought their order. "I couldn't help but over-hear you," he said as he set the girls' teas on the table. "My mother lived in a nursing home. She was so angry with me and my wife when we moved her there. In Portugal, the oldest child looks after the parents."

"Oh?" Juliana said. "It was like that in Opa's home country, too."

Casimiro nodded. "Many European countries used to be that way. Some still are. But we couldn't run the café and take care of her, and private care was too expensive. She was treated well but yes, there were many in the home whose minds had gone. That scared you?"

Juliana nodded.

A kind smile appeared on Casimiro's face. "Think of it more like they're resting, even when they're awake. They lived a long life, maybe even a difficult one. They don't care about the rest of the world anymore. They just want to rest."

Sophie tore open the packaging on her tea bag. "Is it really like that?" She placed the tea bag in her pot.

"I can't tell you for sure," Casimiro said, "but once I

realized that's maybe why so many people look like they have one foot here and one in heaven, I didn't feel so sad."

Another customer called him and he excused himself.

"Actually, I like that," Juliana said.

"So do I."

"I mean, I don't know anything about heaven, but one foot here and one foot...wherever the other side is...I like that. Jasmine said I lived in a bubble because of how much the man scared me."

"You? In a bubble?" Sophie said. "You left all your friends behind, moved here, studied for an entire semester in, like, three weeks, and then Rachel's mom died, and you've had a hard time with dance...I certainly couldn't live your life!" Sophie blew on her tea to cool it.

Juliana smiled as she spoke. "Had you told me a year ago that my life would be like this, I wouldn't have believed it either."

Their teas still hot, Juliana and Sophie lost themselves in conversation in no time.

It was Easter Sunday, and the Schuhmachers, Roths, and Morgans were all at the Morgan household, tapping eggs together.

"My egg will beat yours!" Sophie said to Juliana with glee.

"No, it won't! I'll even bet you another cake or fries or whatever from the café!"

"Or whatever?" Sophie said, a gleam in her eye. "You're on!"

After only three taps, though, Sophie's hard-boiled, bright pink egg cracked Juliana's yellow-with-bunny-stickers egg. Mom didn't have enough onions to peel to dye the eggs.

"I won!" Sophie punched her fists in the air. "I'll take a whole burger!"

Juliana swatted her cousin on the shoulder but she'd make good on her promise. *I'll put it on Opa's tab*, she thought. "I guess I'm eating my egg now," she said.

"Where's one of my brothers or my sister?" Sophie asked as she scanned the room. "I have to beat them."

As Sophie went off in search of a sibling, Juliana headed for the kitchen to peel her egg and place the shells in the green bin.

"You lost, too?" Uncle Peter asked, flashing his usual cheesy smile.

"Yup," Juliana said, pretending to appear dejected. She let out a dramatic sigh for extra effect. "My egg cracked open." She threw the last pieces of shell into the bucket and took a bite. "But at least now I can sit and enjoy it." She smiled.

Uncle Peter bit into his egg. "How are you feeling otherwise?"

"Much better." Should she tell Uncle Peter what she had learned about his coming out and Opa and Oma? Or should she act like she didn't know? Would telling him be too awkward?

"When you keep pushing things down," Uncle Peter said, "they somehow keep coming up. All I can tell you is that life is actually easier when you try to talk to people. It may not seem like it if you're scared to talk about what's bothering you, but that's what happened to me. Brian had it actually worse with his parents."

"Did they come from Japan?" Brian's last name was Yamamoto.

Uncle Peter shook his head while he chewed. "No. They were born here, but they visited family in Japan a lot. They were certainly a conservative family."

"Like Opa and Oma?"

Uncle Peter's body stiffened. Juliana hadn't intended to bring up the topic, she really just wanted to better understand what Uncle Peter meant. But she had to share with him now what she'd learned, awkward or not.

"Mom didn't say anything until I asked directly," she said. "I just put two and two together. And I still love Opa."

Uncle Peter relaxed. "I wouldn't want you not liking him because of his old beliefs."

Juliana swallowed the last of her egg. "To be honest, I haven't had the best beliefs either."

"What do you mean?"

Juliana's face flushed and she stared at the counter as she told Uncle Peter what she'd said about Opa before she'd arrived in Kitchener. "And then when I danced at the nursing home last week, I felt so horrible for having said that."

Uncle Peter put his arm around her. "We're all worried for Tata's future, Juliana. But that's why we're all glad you guys have come back. He's so much happier now, and I'm certainly interested in everything you're learning about my grandmother. He rarely talked about her."

"Mom said that, too. I wonder why?"

Brian waved across the great room at Uncle Peter. Opa walked into the kitchen just as Uncle Peter blew his partner a kiss in front of Opa, and Opa smiled at his son.

"I see you're both talking," he said of his son and grand-daughter. "That's good. That's very good! Family should talk with each other! On Easter! For my birthday! All the time!" He patted Juliana on the head. "That's why my Yulika is back, so she can talk to all of her family." He held up his egg. "Sophie cracked mine," he said, a playful pout on his face.

Juliana and Uncle Peter laughed.

"Sophie, you have a magic egg!" Juliana shouted across the great room.

"And I'm not giving it to you!" Sophie shouted back. A moment later, Mom challenged Sophie to a *titschen* duel.

"Next year, I'm going to ask Katy to boil me a quail egg," Opa declared. "Then no one will beat me!"

"Tata!" Uncle Peter said with feigned anger. "Quail eggs are smaller. That's unfair!"

A mischievous grin appeared on Opa's lips. "Not if we don't tell anyone," he said.

I will definitely put Sophie's order on his tab now, Juliana thought, a big smile on her face.

"Here, have it, Peter. I want a new one. I still have to challenge Brian," Opa said, not noticing Juliana's expression. He passed his unopened but cracked egg to Uncle Peter, reached into the fridge to get a new one for himself, and shuffled back into the crowd.

"We're all lucky to have you here," Uncle Peter said. "I'm sorry the move was so hard on you, but we're really lucky to have you. You actually make this family seem somewhat normal."

At that moment, Juliana caught Dad shaking his belly at Uncle Phillip, who did the same back.

Uncle Peter followed her gaze. "Are they seriously comparing belly fat?"

Juliana tried to stifle her giggle. Her dad had no qualms about shaking his spare tire, especially to embarrass her. But Uncle Phillip, too?

"Yup," she managed to squeeze past her lips.

"They married into the family," Uncle Peter said. "They don't count."

Juliana and Uncle Peter burst out laughing, doubling over, their arms wrapped around their own bellies. By the time they calmed down and could stand straight again, everyone was staring at them, which only caused them to double over again.

So this is what family feels like, Juliana thought as she calmed down a second time.

Across the room, she spotted Opa beaming. She would never forget that smile so long as she lived.

SETTING THE RECORD STRAIGHT

Between Worlds tells a contemporary fictional story together with a story that is historical fiction. In both parts of the book, I've taken facts about life in the time period in which the story is set and included them in a fictional story. In writing novels, the story always comes first (because otherwise this would be a history textbook), so this section explains any important facts that may have been changed to fit the story and adds more background to the story. If you have any questions about what you've read in this or any of the other books in the series, ask away! My contact information is in the "Stay in Touch!" section.

LARGE GATHERINGS IN SEMLAK

Much of the lifestyle in Semlak at the time was a closed circuit: everything was reused, food scraps were fed to farm animals, everyone had their own well, etc. I don't know any details about upper class society in Semlak, but without plastic, there was very little waste to begin with. (I believe garbage made of metal, though, was dumped on the outskirts of the village.)

That also meant that large gatherings, like Easter celebrations, didn't produce a lot of waste. Because most families only had enough dishes for themselves and perhaps one more family over as guests, families invited to larger gatherings brought their own dishes. This might seem rude to us in North America, because it would suggest that the host's dishes weren't sanitary enough to eat from, but it was a matter of practicality and politeness in Semlak.

After everyone ate, the women washed the dishes. Because households did not have running water at this time, fresh water was brought in from the well, and dishes were washed in large, porcelain bowls with homemade soap.

DID WOUNDED MEN WORK AFTER THE WAR?

World War One was the first war where millions of wounded men returned *en masse* and not all were not able to take up their former employment. This happened in all countries that sent men off to fight. Men could not find meaningful work because of disfigurement, physical injury, and psychological trauma. However, life had to move forward, and many of these men were forgotten by their families, often leaving them begging in the streets, especially in cities. Stefan's story is not representative of Semlak specifically but of many veterans of WWI.

I believe men's health was rarely spoken about in families. When I came across first-hand accounts of WWI from Germans of Eastern Europe or second-hand accounts from their children, I continually heard the same sentence: "He was not the same man when he came back." That was all they could say.

COULDN'T MEN GET COUNSELLING?

Psychology and psychiatry were in their infancy at this time, and these doctors worked in cities where there were more people who needed help. Without the speed of the Internet, scientific knowledge also spread slowly. Another factor was a general attitude that humans could control all aspects of their brains, which we now know isn't true. This is the basis for Georg's story. If you've begun the series with this book, read *Between Worlds 4: What Friends Do* next, where Elisabeth struggles to understand why Georg is the way he is.

OPA'S EMPHASIS ON RUBBER WORKERS

This aspect of Juliana's story helps make the series unique to Kitchener, Waterloo, and Cambridge, the three cities in Waterloo Region, where I live. Waterloo Region also has three townships, but their main industry has historically been farming. When Opa jabs at a double-page spread in *The Waterloo Region Record*, our local daily paper, he's referring to something that was actually published.

Waterloo Region housed numerous factories that produced rubber over the decades. Opa's house is close to one. In 2019/2020, Greg Mercer of *The Waterloo Region Record* wrote numerous articles exposing the dangers these factory workers faced, including abnormally high levels of cancer. The newspaper published this two-page spread of former workers from these factories who'd died of this horrible illness. I was shocked to recognize many faces.

My grandparents used to work at one such factory, with my grandfather on the floor and my grandmother in the canteen. My grandfather died in his 60s from a stroke, and although my grandmother developed cancer, she lived another 30 years cancer-free. The stories in *The Record* really opened my eyes to what my grandparents endured, not only as immigrants, but as a factory worker and food services worker.

Occupational hazards are very real for many people.

Thanks to a grant I received from the Region of Waterloo Arts Fund, *Between Worlds 8* will dive deeper into this story.

STAY IN TOUCH!

If you enjoyed the book, sign up for my monthly newsletter! I write it myself, so it's my words to you. You'll get the following:

- Sneak peeks at upcoming books
- Updates about online and in-person appearances
- Book and writing recommendations
- Recipes I love
- Contests
- And more!

Visit BetweenWorldsYA.com to sign up!

Prefer social media? All my links are listed under my bio, at the end of the book.

ACKNOWLEDGEMENTS

No book is a project completed by one person. I'd like to thank the following for helping me with this book:

- My best friend, Annamae, for talking to me about the changes in high school since we were students.
- George Broughton & Susan Parks-Broughton of All Things Tea in Belmont Village for their support and creative marketing ideas during the pandemic, which hit us just as I was about to launch *Between Worlds 6: Missing Home*.
- Chris at Words Worth Books in Waterloo for his continued support with book sales through the pandemic.
- Lois Raats, business consultant extraordinaire, for helping me pivot my book plans during the pandemic.
- Mrs. Rossweiler, a Danube Swabian in her 100s who took the time to tell me about her

memories of life as a German in Eastern Europe.

- Anne Dreer, a younger Danube Swabian who not only helped connect me to Mrs. Rossweiler but also shared numerous stories with me.
- Research for these novels comes from numerous sources. However, I'd like to especially thank Georg Schmidt for curating the book *Semlak;* Gabriela Rat and Crenguta Nicolae in Romania, and Daniel Kalman and Levente Csibi in Hungary for their more in-depth research; the many volunteers of Donauschwaben Villages Helping Hands; and Henry Fischer for his research on Lutheran Germans in the Banat.
- My grandparents, for all their stories.
- My street team, who sees earlier drafts of marketing materials and the manuscript and offers feedback: Rachel, Florentina, Jean Tacey Hagen, She Whose Name Did Not Need to Be Mentioned, Jonnathan Straus, Khristopher Straus, Corey Straus, Liz, and Claudette.
- Heather Wright, my consulting editor and writing coach, who helped me at the conceptual stage of the book and encouraged me throughout the full project.
- Susan Fish, my reviewer and copy editor, who showed me where I still needed to improve the

plot and then helped me smooth out my language. Any remaining errors are mine.

- Michelle Fairbanks of Fresh Design for the cover and many of my marketing materials.
- Mom, Dad, and Kristin, for all their years of dealing with my writerly moods! And of course for all their love and support today with these books.
- Deardra King-Leslie, my dance teacher. Without her, Juliana would not be a dancer.
- ali macgee, my mentor, for her continued support in my writing career.
- Corey, Khristopher, and Jonnathan, for dealing with my writerly moods now in my adult years! And also for backing me up and encouraging me to keep working.

This list keeps getting longer, as you can see, and I'm so very grateful to everyone for helping me with this journey.

ABOUT LORI

Photo by Erin Watt Photography

Lori Wolf-Heffner is a former competitive dancer, dance teacher, and theatre manager. She was a member of the first Canadian National Tap Team, back in 1996, under the leadership of Bonnie Dyer, with choreographer Mathew Clark. She's written for *Dance Canada Quarterly*, *just dance!* magazine, and *The Dance Current* (all under Lori Straus).

Fluent in German, Lori lived in Germany for three years, never once realizing just how close she was to some of the villages her ancestors left to migrate to Eastern Europe in the 1700s.

Lori lives in Waterloo, Ontario, Canada, with her husband and two sons. She is a member of The Writers' Union of Canada and the Alliance of Independent Authors.

facebook.com/loriwolfheffner

x.com/LoriWolfHeffner

instagram.com/loriwolfheffner

goodreads.com/lori_wolf-heffner

bookbub.com/author/lori-wolf-heffner

pinterest.com/loriwolfheffner

amazon.com/author/loriwolfheffner

9 781989 465158